"Stay the Night, Rae,"

Jonathan said. "You won't regret it."

"Oh, Jonathan." Her voice was full of her own needs.

Lifting his head, he stared down at her, his cynically triumphant smile piercing the layers of desire he had woven around her. Rae tore herself from his arms as the glitter of triumph vanished from his eyes. Her mantle of cool disdain, cultivated over the years, fell into place.

She spoke with haughty coldness. "The one thing I would regret most is staying the night with you. You're already my business tutor. I don't think I want you to teach me anything else."

Hurriedly she made her escape.

MARGARET RIPY
loves to travel and only writes about places she has visited. In her books there is a "little bit of herself and her experiences." Without the support and love of Mike, her husband of thirteen years, she says her writing wouldn't be possible. He has the characteristics she wants in a male hero.

Dear Reader,

Silhouette Special Editions are an exciting new line of contemporary romances from Silhouette Books. Special Editions are written specifically for our readers who want a story with heightened romantic tension.

Special Editions have all the elements you've enjoyed in Silhouette Romances and *more*. These stories concentrate on romance in a longer, more realistic and sophisticated way, and they feature greater sensual detail.

I hope you enjoy this book and all the wonderful romances from Silhouette.

Karen Solem
Editor-in-Chief
Silhouette Books

MARGARET RIPY
A Matter of Pride

Silhouette Special Edition
Published by Silhouette Books New York
America's Publisher of Contemporary Romance

Other Silhouette Books by Margaret Ripy

A Second Chance on Love
The Flaming Tree
A Treasure of Love
Tomorrow's Memory
Rainy Day Dreams

SILHOUETTE BOOKS, a Division of Simon & Schuster, Inc.
1230 Avenue of the Americas, New York, N.Y. 10020

Copyright © 1983 by Margaret Ripy

Distributed by Pocket Books

ISBN: 0-671-53634-6

First Silhouette Books printing December, 1983

10 9 8 7 6 5 4 3 2 1

Map by Ray Lundgren

America's Publisher of Contemporary Romance

Printed in the U.S.A.

To Gaye and Bob Young—
Thank you for your support and help

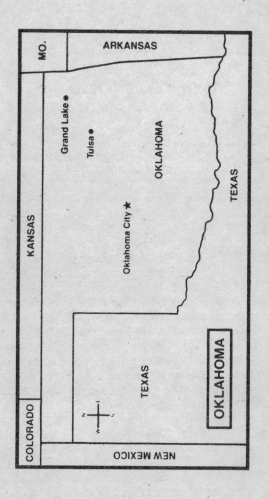

Chapter One

$\mathcal{M}$r. King, here are the reports you wanted."

Jonathan King's executive assistant handed him a folder with HAMILTON OIL stamped on it. Jonathan's brow furrowed as he read through the reports on the oil company he had invested in heavily. He had two choices—sell his shares or take over the controlling interest. Usually he would jump at the chance to take over a company, but he had been restless lately. Everything was so easy now; there were few challenges anymore.

Jonathan flipped the folder closed in a gesture of boredom. "What's your opinion, Bill? Do you think Hamilton Oil is worth my time and money?"

"With your help, Raymond Hamilton almost had the company out of the financial trouble it was in during the late seventies. The future of the company looks good, Mr. King, especially now with the excellent incentives to explore for oil and gas." Bill Woods sat across from Jonathan in King Industries' Lear jet.

"Raymond's son inherits the company. I believe Ray Hamilton is a drilling engineer working his way up through the ranks of his father's company." Jonathan glanced toward the window and noticed the jet descending through the clouds. "And now he owns the company—at least part of it," he added in a whisper.

Never before had indecision taken such a hold on Jonathan. It would be a good move for him to buy the controlling interest in the company as stipulated in his agreement with Raymond, but maybe he should give Raymond's son a chance to make it on his own. Jonathan was sure Raymond's life insurance would help the young man come up with the necessary money to buy Jonathan's thirty-five percent, but it would still take time for the young man to raise that kind of money. Did he want to gamble during that time with his shares? Jonathan asked himself. In the oil business money could be made quickly and lost quickly.

Since the company was doing better lately, it would have only been a matter of a few years before Raymond himself had bought back the shares he had sold Jonathan. It had been Raymond's wish to keep the company in the family, and in the year and a half Jonathan had been associated with him, he had grown to respect the older man.

Suddenly Jonathan reached a decision. He would meet Raymond's son and determine if he thought the young man was capable of running Hamilton Oil without him. If so, he would hold on to his shares until Ray Hamilton could buy back his thirty-five percent. But if he thought Ray couldn't manage the company effectively, he would step in and buy the sixteen percent necessary to control it. He would protect his investment. It was one thing to be a drilling engineer and another the head of a company, overseeing all the operations, especially the financial end of the business.

Jonathan yawned and closed his eyes, slouching down deep into his seat. He had finally learned the value of resting and relaxing. For years, especially after his father's death, he had worked so hard, putting in long hours seven days a week, that he had almost burned himself out. Only in the last year had he slowed down. He could now enjoy his hobbies of skydiving and scuba diving, but there was still something lacking. There were few challenges in the business world for him now, and again he had to acknowledge he was restless, bored.

"After the funeral, Bill, I want to see Hamilton Oil's books; then in a few days I want a meeting set up between myself and Ray Hamilton." As the jet touched the ground at Tulsa International, Jonathan added, "Cancel any business meetings I have in Dallas for the next ten days. I think I'll drive up to my cabin on Grand Lake for a few days before I conclude my business with Raymond's son."

Jonathan hadn't been to Grand Lake in at least two years. In fact, he rarely came to Tulsa anymore, not since he had moved the main offices of King Industries to Dallas after his father's death thirteen years ago.

He maintained his family home in Tulsa, but it was mostly used by the other members of his family. His mother often visited old friends in Tulsa, and his younger sister occasionally flew in from New York or Europe to stay for a week or two at the cabin or in town.

A frown deepened the lines on Jonathan's tanned face as he combed his fingers through his thick brown hair. What was he going to do about Carole? Only last week he had paid off a tabloid reporter to keep a damaging report out of his cheap paper. Carole was so flighty; she did things without thinking, living for the moment's pleasure. If he had his way, he would let Carole face the consequences of her actions, but it would kill his mother if she found out about all of Carole's little "escapades." Vanessa King was like a china doll—delicate and very fragile. Jonathan had promised his father before his death that he would protect his mother at all costs.

But dammit! It ate into him when he had to pay blackmailers to shield his mother. It went against all he stood for. But Carole would hear about it this weekend. She was coming to Tulsa with a friend, and he would make it very clear to his sister that she would have to change her ways or there would be no more money from him. With no allowance she would have a hard time living it up.

"Mr. King, the car's waiting," Bill said, breaking into Jonathan's thoughts.

Jonathan looked at his watch, then at his assistant. "We'd better go straight to the cemetery or we'll be late for the funeral."

Jonathan scanned the group assembled at the grave site. Who was Ray Hamilton Jr.? he wondered, again going over in his mind the funeral service at the chapel. The only people sitting in the family section were a young woman, an older man next to her and a middle-aged couple. Surely Raymond's son was attending the funeral.

Jonathan's gaze fixed upon the young woman moving toward the coffin. She placed a single white rose on it, then stepped back and stood next to the older man again. Who was this woman to Raymond Hamilton? He only had one child. Had Raymond married recently? Jonathan had been in Europe the last six weeks and it was possible that Raymond had married without his knowledge. It wasn't that unusual for a young woman to marry a man twice her age, especially if she thought the man was rich.

With a sharp, cynical look he quickly appraised the young woman. Her hair was like molten lava and her eyes were a light shade, probably gray or blue, fringed with long black lashes which made her eyes seem even larger than they were. Black was a flattering color on her, a perfect foil for her ivory complexion. At a leisurely pace his gaze traveled the length of her shapely body, clad in a black tailored suit. *Very attractive,* he thought, noting the full, firm breasts, the slim waist and the long, slender legs. Even at a distance Jonathan sensed an air of determination and elegance about the woman which instantly intrigued him.

The minister had finished the service and the people were leaving. A woman near Jonathan turned to her husband and said, "We have to offer our condolences to Ray before we leave."

Instantly alert, Jonathan watched as the couple approached the young woman with the short auburn hair. Ray? He was confused. Was Ray a woman? The few times Raymond had spoken about his only child he had always called him (or her?) Ray. Jonathan had just assumed the "Ray" was male and hadn't thought much else about it. After all, drilling engineers were usually men and an oil rig was no place for a lady.

Jonathan moved closer to the couple talking to the woman and listened. If she was Raymond's heir, he would have to reevaluate his position.

"I'm sorry about your father, Rae. If we can do anything to help you, let us know," the older woman said.

"Thank you, Ruth. I have everything under control, but I appreciate your offer," Rae answered, her gaze darting past the couple to the tall stranger behind them.

There was something familiar about the man. Then suddenly Rae remembered observing him leaving her father's office about six months ago. She had wondered then who he was, but some business had demanded her immediate concentration and the opportunity had never arisen for her to ask her father.

"Rae, are you all right?"

Ruth's question pulled Rae's attention back to the couple standing before her. "I'm fine. Thank you for coming."

Rae was tired and needed to sit down. She hadn't had a moment to herself since her father's death had been announced, and she valued her privacy. Everyone was being so kind, but right now all she wanted was to be alone.

The older couple left and the stranger now faced her with his hand extended. His fingers slowly closed over hers, the touch searing as they shook hands.

Jonathan's gaze locked with Rae's. Her eyes were gray, dark now with her emotions and the long, tiring day.

For a few seconds Rae allowed herself the luxury of her hand being cradled in his strong one. His skin next to hers felt rough, as though he had often worked with his hands. But strangely, she sensed a gentleness in his grip as well.

"I'm Jonathan King, Miss Hamilton." He waited for a reaction to his name, but there was none. He knew Raymond had wanted their partnership kept a secret and obviously he had, even from his own daughter. This was going to prove very interesting, Jonathan decided, his curiosity aroused. "I was a—business associate of your father's from Dallas."

"It was nice of you to come all that way for his funeral," she replied politely, finally taking her hand from his. Why did she feel as if she had been burned merely by his touch?

Jonathan King? There was a familiar ring to his name. "Are you in the oil industry, Mr. King?"

"Among other things, Miss Hamilton. My corporation is into many fields. Your father's death will be a loss to the city. I was originally from Tulsa and have heard a great deal about the things he has done for the city."

"He didn't think there was a nicer place on the face of this earth."

"I was shocked to hear of his death. The last time I saw him he was bragging about winning a tennis match three sets to two."

The soft breeze ruffled her hair, and Rae brushed a strand away from her cheek. "He pushed himself too hard. He had a heart attack while fishing. Dad's doctor tried to warn him to slow down, that his age would catch up with him one day. But Dad thought he was invincible, and would never listen to anyone." Her voice thickened with the pain of her loss, and a lump formed in her throat. She had meant to be as strong as her father would have wished, and here she was breaking down in front of a stranger. But there was a gentle quality to his voice that unnerved her, disarming the shield she placed around her inner thoughts.

Jonathan King was ruggedly handsome with brown hair and piercing black eyes that reached into a person's soul and sought its innermost thoughts. His presence was commanding, his appearance utterly male and virile. This was a man who left his mark wherever he went; he would be a formidable opponent, and she immediately hoped she would never be on his opposing side.

"May I walk you to your limousine, Miss Hamilton? You look as if you need to escape for a while." His voice was low, his words meant only for her.

Rae glanced beyond Jonathan and saw several other couples waiting nearby. Suddenly she wanted to be by herself. The last few days had drained her emotionally, and she felt she had to escape the good intentions of everyone to be alone at least for a couple of hours before facing all that needed to be done.

"Yes, please."

Jonathan slid his arm about her in a protective gesture. Rae was touched. She had had so little of that in her twenty-eight years that she wasn't sure how to react. She wanted to lean into this stranger's strength and let his arm stay about her in a comforting embrace. But as they neared the black limousine, Rae instinctively moved away and turned to thank him.

"Good day, Miss Hamilton."

His voice was deep and husky, and she liked the sound of it. She nodded, then climbed into the car.

As the limousine pulled away, Jonathan stood on the side of the road and watched it disappear around a curve. He should have known better than to assume anything. That could cost him dearly in the business world. He wanted to know everything about Rae Hamilton because they would soon be working side by side. He had decided to buy the controlling shares in Hamilton Oil. His interest was definitely aroused and that hadn't happened in a long time. He sensed a challenge in the form of Rae Hamilton and he wasn't one to turn his back on a challenge, nor to lose one.

Rae paced back and forth in her father's study, her strides rigid. Pausing at the bay window, she stared unseeing at the quickly darkening sky. Her father had been dead over a week; yet at any moment she expected him to come walking through the door, his dynamic presence dominating the room.

The sound of the door opening caused Rae to spin around to face the older man who entered the study. "Mrs. Madison told me you were in here. No doubt working late for the fourth night in a row."

Rae sagged against the windowsill. "Oh, Carl, you scared me." For just a second she had imagined this nightmarish week had been a dream and she was waking up to find her father returning home from his fishing expedition.

Pushing herself away from the windowsill, Rae walked to her father's desk and sat down behind it. "What can I do for you?"

"You can stop working so hard and go home."

"I can't, Carl. There's so much to do."

Carl sat across from her with a determined look on his face. "And it will be here tomorrow morning."

"Tomorrow is Monday and I have my first staff meeting scheduled. It has to be finished tonight." For the first time since her father's death, Rae genuinely smiled. "I only have a little more work, so rest assured I'll be leaving in an hour."

"Why are you working here, anyway, Rae?"

Carl Lawson was an old, dear friend of the family who had been like an uncle as she had grown up. She had always been able to talk to Carl, something she had never been allowed to do with her own father. That thought carved a frown deep into Rae's features.

"I'm not sure, Carl. Perhaps unconsciously I thought I'd receive some guidance from my father. There's a lot that's unfamiliar to me. I was out in the field a lot this last year and am not as acquainted with the other aspects of the business as I should be in order to take it over." For a moment she permitted her insecurity to show in her wide gray eyes, then quickly concealed her uncertainty. As always, she wouldn't let her father down. By giving her the company he had loved so much, he had placed a great deal of faith in her, and she would live up to his expectations.

"Over the years I've sat back and watched you grow into a beautiful young woman, Rae. Duty and responsibility should be important to everyone, but with you they are an obsession. There are more things in life than Hamilton Oil and your work. There—"

"Carl, don't. I know you mean well, but I'm content with my life. I love my work and Dad—" Rae suddenly stood, unable to express her feelings, even to Carl. "Really, Carl, I do have a lot to see to and I'm tired. It's been a long week."

"Very well."

Carl rose, his face lined with his exhaustion. He had been with her since the beginning. The small boat her father had been fishing in had been found a week ago last Wednesday, but there had been no trace of Raymond Hamilton. Rae had known her father was dead even before the authorities finally found his body in the lake on Thursday afternoon.

After showing Carl to the door, Rae leaned against the cool wood and scanned her elegant surroundings. She had always visited her father with mixed feelings; this was the house she had grown up in, but it had never been a home to her.

Walking across the spacious foyer, Rae stepped back into her father's study. The numbness of her father's death had finally been replaced with weariness and that ever-present sense of duty to her father. He would have scorned her if she had allowed herself the luxury of tears. He would have told her the mourners were only feeling sorry for themselves, not the person who was dead. Life must go on as before. Wasn't that what he had done when her mother had died twelve years ago? Rae had learned long ago that her father was a hard man to please. She had spent most of her life trying to please him, always trying to make up for the fact that she hadn't been a boy. Even though her father had never openly said anything, somehow she had felt responsible for being the wrong sex. And she had felt she had never truly lived up to his high expectations for her.

Rae collapsed into the chair behind her father's desk and surveyed the pile of paperwork on it. She knew what her father would expect her to do—put his death behind her and quickly familiarize herself with every aspect of Hamilton Oil. "The king is dead, long live the queen," she whispered in a quaking voice.

Chapter Two

Sighing, Rae placed her pen on the desk, closed the folder and leaned back in the chair. The taut strain that had gripped her slowly flowed away as she forced herself to relax for the first time that day.

A knock at the study door startled her, and Rae immediately sat up straight. "Yes?"

Mrs. Madison opened the door and peered inside. "There's a Mr. King here to see you."

The stranger from the funeral? Why was he here? "Please show him in, Mrs. Madison."

When Jonathan King entered the study, Rae was once again keenly aware of the potent power that emanated from the man. His penetrating gaze caught hers and held it across the expanse of the room, a silence stretching between them as they assessed each other.

Glancing away, Rae severed the magnetic spell and rose slowly, buying time while she brought her riotous emotions under control. It was her distraught state over her father's death and the tremendous weight of the job ahead of her that made her legs weak and her heartbeat accelerate—not the dark gleam in this stranger's eyes which had flamed for a few seconds before he had disguised the raw sensuality of that mind-stunning look.

She had risen and walked in front of her desk before she encountered his frank appraisal again, a neutral expression now on his face. "What can I do for you, Mr. King?"

"Jonathan, please. And it's not what you can do for me, but what I can do for you." There was a smile in his voice that charmed her senses.

Arching a brow, she leveled an amused look at him. "And what could that possibly be?"

"Dinner. One glance at you and I can see you've neglected to eat or sleep much this last week."

"Very perceptive. But I've had other things on my mind."

"Those other things won't mean much if you become ill."

She automatically brought her hand to her hair to smooth it. "Do I look *that* bad?"

A very appreciative male gleam flickered in the depths of his black eyes as they roamed over her. "On the contrary. But I see exhaustion in those large gray eyes."

Why did she feel it would be hard to hide

much from this man? She wasn't used to anyone reading her so well. Very early in life it had become a defensive maneuver to wall her true emotions up inside and present a cool, efficient facade to the world. It had pleased her father that she wasn't as her mother had been—clinging, dependent and emotional.

"I still don't understand why you stopped by this house. I don't live here," she said, her voice soft and flowing.

Jonathan simply replied, "I know."

In fact, he knew a lot about Rae Sinclair Hamilton. The detailed report he had read on her this morning at his cabin on Grand Lake revealed a woman of many facets and contradictions. The report had only served to spur his interest even more. She had worked for her father ever since graduating from the University of Oklahoma's engineering school six years ago, but she had maintained her own apartment and complete independence.

Her father had obviously respected her engineering knowledge and had let her make the final decisions in that area of the business. That in itself said a lot for her, since Raymond Hamilton had been known for his ruthlessness. If Raymond hadn't tried to expand so rapidly in the late seventies, he wouldn't have had to look for a silent partner two years ago. Raymond Hamilton's only mistake would cost him the company. For Jonathan was also aware that Rae knew next to nothing about managing a business, especially the financial aspects of one, and he didn't intend to let her experiment with his money.

"Why did you stop by here, Mr. King?" Rae repeated her question, caught by the purposefulness in his expression.

Jonathan shrugged. "My house isn't too far from here. I saw the lights on in the study and gambled you would be working late." He spread his arms wide, an engaging grin suddenly appearing on his face which softened his hard features. "So here I am."

Rae sensed Jonathan never gambled, that when he wanted something he made certain it was a sure thing. "Thank you for your offer, but I've just finished a whole day's paperwork and I really am tired. I'm going to drive home, grab a quick bite and fall into bed."

His smile widened. "That's your problem."

"What?"

"Grabbing a quick bite. You need to completely relax over a leisurely dinner. A glass of wine and a good meal would do wonders for you."

For some unexplained reason his offer was tempting. She had denied herself so much in the last ten years. Her work and the company had required most of her time in the past, and now they would even more. She hadn't been prepared to run the company. Her father had wanted her to work up through the ranks, and his death had been so unexpected that she felt like a fish floundering on land. Would she ever be back in her own element?

"Rae, I have a dinner at home waiting for me that I'm sure will be enough for two. It will be quiet, private and relaxing."

It was everything she wanted, coupled with

the company of another human being, which she needed right now. For the last week she had been left alone—too alone—as she faced the fact that her father was gone and she had been left in charge without the required expertise. But she was determined to do her best and make Hamilton Oil bigger and better. She knew she could do it. Hadn't she already become a successful drilling engineer, respected by her peers in a male-dominated profession.

"Let me get my purse and sweater. I'll follow you to your house."

His house was only a few blocks from her father's in the affluent Utica Square area where large, beautiful homes with spacious lawns spoke of great wealth. And Jonathan King's was one of the largest and most elegant houses in the area. Several times she had driven past his house on the way to her father's and wondered what the inside was like. Of course, she hadn't voiced her speculations aloud and it had always remained a mystery.

Rae parked her midsized sedan, which was still dirty with red clay from her trip to western Oklahoma two weeks ago, next to Jonathan's silver Mercedes coupe. *What a contrast,* she thought as she slid from her car, straightening to meet Jonathan's eyes studying her from only a foot away. In that instant she sensed they would be more than acquaintances. She felt their future together would hold a deep, intimate relationship and she turned to leave before it was too late.

Jonathan saw the frightened look flash in

her eyes and reached out to capture her wrist in a gentle manacle. "I called ahead. My housekeeper has already set an extra place."

Underneath his polite words Rae knew he was telling her that she couldn't back out, not when she was in front of his house. She was in his domain now. "I can't stay long." Then something compelled her to explain further. "I have my first staff meeting early tomorrow morning and I want to be fresh and ready."

"I can remember my first staff meeting." A wry smile crept over his face. "It is a little disarming at first."

Rae glanced toward Jonathan as they climbed the steps to his front door. "Somehow I can't see anything unnerving you."

Stepping into the lighted foyer, Jonathan laughed. "I've learned a lot since I was twenty-three. I didn't have the time I needed to work for my father's company. I had just finished law school when he died."

I didn't have the time either, Rae thought, and felt a kinship with this man. He had obviously succeeded in taking over and learning the ropes of management successfully, and that thought made her relax slightly.

"Do you have any advice to impart?" She asked it jokingly, but underneath the light tone it was apparent she genuinely wanted an answer.

"Listen and then listen some more. You can learn a lot from the people around you, but in the end it is *your* decision that's final."

And that was what scared her so. Would she make the right decisions? Would she go after the right land leases? Would she know when to take a calculated risk? So much money was involved in drilling for oil and gas that it wouldn't take many wrong decisions to ruin the company.

"But I didn't persuade you to join me for dinner to talk business. Let that wait until tomorrow morning, Rae."

Her name came so easily to his lips. It sounded like the most natural thing for him to say, as if he had been doing it for years.

"What would you like a drink before dinner?" Jonathan asked while he guided her toward the living room.

"That glass of wine you spoke of sounds fine."

"A Chablis?"

"Yes, thank you."

While Jonathan poured her wine and fixed himself a Scotch on the rocks, Rae surveyed the living room done in beige and hunter's-green. The room was huge, the length of the house, with French doors leading outside, probably to a terrace or a garden. The ceiling was high, giving the room a very open, airy feeling. The marble fireplace, the rich oak of the bar, the masterpieces on the walls and the luxurious furnishings indicated great wealth. But then Rae didn't have to see his home to know he was a very successful businessman; he had that quiet air of authority about him.

"Here. Now, sit and relax," Jonathan said, handing her a wineglass.

She gladly obeyed, weariness weaving through her mind and body. So many figures and facts had been crammed into her mind the last few days that she wondered if she would remember any tomorrow morning. And there was so much to do in the next few days besides the staff meeting. There was the reading of the will, the examination of the books . . .

"Well, well, brother dear, who is this?" a young woman said from the doorway. Rae looked up to find the woman advancing into the room.

"I thought you had a date tonight," Jonathan said, his tone hard, his eyes dark slits.

"Now, I'm glad Bradley had to be late. I always love meeting one of your lady friends."

The young woman sat across from Rae on one of the beige-and-green-printed couches. She was wearing a very revealing dress of shimmering satin, which lent a richness to the room and made Rae acutely aware of her jeans.

"Rae, I must apologize for my sister's behavior. Carole can be very rude at times."

Carole's laughter filled the charged silence. "Oh, Jonathan, do you think you're going to spend your whole life apologizing for me?"

"No, because after our talk Friday I'm sure you know where I'm coming from."

"I could earn my own money," Carole retorted.

This time Jonathan was the one to laugh. "You work! I don't think you know what the word means."

"Then perhaps I could marry money. Bradley has enough for my expensive tastes."

Fascinated, Rae watched this verbal exchange between brother and sister. Jonathan was angry at his younger sister, but underneath his gruff exterior Rae sensed a deep family love. It was all right if he criticized his sister, but he wouldn't tolerate anyone else doing it. Carole enjoyed teasing her brother, but Rae saw a respect for him lurking in his sister's eyes when she looked at Jonathan.

"Good. Then Bradley can handle you."

"Or I could handle him," Carole said in a flippant voice. Rising and turning to Rae, Jonathan's sister continued in a very proper, ladylike tone, "It was so nice to meet you, Rae . . ."

"Hamilton."

Surprise widened Carole's brown eyes. "Hamilton Oil?"

"Yes."

Jonathan was on his feet, his hand clasped around Carole's upper arm as he escorted her toward the door. "I hear the doorbell. No doubt Bradley. We wouldn't want you to keep him waiting."

"He's used to that." Carole yanked her arm free and was turning back toward Rae. "You answer the door, Jonathan. If I did . . . now, that would shock poor Bradley. He's never seen me be on time."

"No way, sister dear." A menacing calm touched Jonathan's voice. "You take care of your own date."

"While you take care of yours." Carole glanced over Jonathan's shoulder to say, "Good night, Rae."

A fine-tuned tension held Jonathan in the doorway until Bradley had shut the front door and they were gone. Carole knew about his partnership with Raymond Hamilton and he knew she would have said something to Rae. He didn't want Rae to find out until tomorrow; he wanted nothing between them until then. He wanted to get to know Rae. It would make it easier for him to handle her later, he told himself firmly. That was the only reason he had driven by her father's house after calling her apartment and receiving no answer. It wasn't because her image had haunted him the whole week. He rejected that reason as he rejected the idea of letting her try to run the company on her own. She didn't have the knowledge needed.

"Do you have any more brothers or sisters, Jonathan?"

He swung around and walked back to the couch. "No, thank God. One is enough."

"I always wanted a brother or sister to play —and fight—with when I was growing up." There was a loneliness in her voice as she reflected on her childhood.

"And there have been times I've wished I was an only child." Jonathan forced a lightness into the conversation.

"Why is it that people always wish for what they don't have?"

"It's like the horse that cranes its neck to eat the grass on the other side of the fence."

The rich timbre of Rae's laughter filled Jonathan with an inner warmth. It was nice to see her smile and laugh. Suddenly he wished there could be more times like this after she had gotten over her father's death; but by tomorrow afternoon she would hate him. It had been foolish of him to mix business with pleasure. He had his own family to think of and his taking over Hamilton Oil was strictly a business affair.

An older, gray-haired man appeared in the doorway. "Do you want dinner served now, sir?"

"Yes, that would be fine, Samuel. Just place the dishes on the table and that will be all for the evening." When his butler left, Jonathan continued while escorting Rae from the room. "I usually eat in the morning room where it's much more informal. The dining room is so large and overwhelming. Two people would look lost eating in there."

Jonathan motioned toward the dining room as they passed the door. The room was indeed large, with a table that seated sixteen. In comparison, the morning room was quite small, with a warm, cheerful atmosphere that Rae instantly liked. She would have eaten all her meals in a room like this one. However, the dining room would be safer, Rae acknowledged to herself. The morning room wasn't only informal but intimate as well.

As Jonathan assisted her into a comfortable, brown leather chair, then sat next to her, Rae eyed the dishes before her. Prime rib, a sweet potato casserole, asparagus in a lemon sauce and a tossed green salad weren't her idea of a simple dinner for one.

"Are you sure you didn't have this all planned in advance?" she asked with a laugh.

"What gave me away?" Amusement danced in his eyes.

"A lot of thought went into this meal and there's so much. Is anyone else joining us?"

"No. It's only you and I."

A shiver moved up Rae's spine at the provocative way Jonathan had said, "It's only you and I," and the morning room became even smaller, more intimate.

"Why?"

Jonathan didn't need to ask what she meant by the simple question. He knew. He felt her confusion as if an electrical current had flowed from her through him. In fact, in the last few hours he had asked himself that same question many times. Why had he wanted to see Rae Hamilton tonight? Did he want to remember one night when Hamilton Oil wouldn't stand between them?

In a low, husky whisper he said, "I couldn't forget your large gray eyes."

It wasn't a lie. The vulnerability in her eyes at the funeral had reached out to him and plagued him this last week. He was equally aware that she hadn't been conscious of the look she had turned on him after scanning the people waiting to see her. He hadn't seen that expression again and doubted he would; Rae Hamilton rarely showed she was vulnerable to the world.

Jonathan King was so different from the men she was used to that Rae didn't know what to say to his answer. So she simply replied, "Well, this looks delicious." Then she began dishing the food onto her plate and passing the bowls to Jonathan.

For an hour Rae forgot everything but the man next to her as they talked about various topics ranging from the ballet to the Dallas Cowboys. No unpleasant subjects intruded on their dinner, and by the time they were finished they were both relaxed and sated.

"You were right, Jonathan."

"Naturally. All my women tell me that." He grinned as he sat back in his chair.

Ignoring his teasing comment, she continued, "This dinner and the wine were just what I needed. Now, I think I can go home and sleep like a baby till tomorrow morning."

He leaned forward and clasped her hand. A tingling glow spread quickly up her arm from the touch. "You haven't been sleeping well. That's understandable, Rae."

She didn't try to hide the fact that she had spent most nights pacing her bedroom. So much had been placed on her shoulders when her father had died. She didn't even have the time to grieve for his death. The company had come first in her father's life and now must come first in hers. Too many people depended on her.

"My life has changed drastically since my father's death and will continue to do so."

"And the unknown can be frightening," Jonathan finished for her.

The gentleness in his voice, the tenderness in his eyes were chipping away at her wall of reserve. If only she could tell someone what she was really thinking, voice her doubts and confusion. But a lifelong habit couldn't be broken in one hour.

Rae withdrew her hand from his and rose. "It's getting late and I'd better be leaving."

"I've enjoyed this evening, Rae." And he meant every word. Rae Hamilton fascinated him. He hadn't felt this way in a long time. His restlessness was slipping away to be replaced with an eagerness for the hunt, for at this moment he felt like a predator. He wanted Rae badly, and he gladly welcomed the challenge of conquering her and making her come alive. Somehow he would find a way to mix business with pleasure.

Outside, Jonathan opened Rae's car door for her, but before she could escape into her sedan, he halted her with a hand on her wrist. Transfixed, Rae was helpless to stop what she knew would come next—perhaps because she wanted him to kiss her.

Jonathan laced his fingers through her auburn hair and pulled her toward him. The seeking exploration of his lips grew into a persuasive insistence, his tongue plunging into her mouth, meeting hers in a duel. Rae centered her world on that kiss as she matched him in an ardent response. His tantalizing closeness was the balm she needed, and she didn't want to part.

One hand untangled from her hair and wandered to the sensitive flesh of her neck, lightly stroking the line of her throat. Then his mouth left hers to trail light kisses to her earlobe where she felt his teeth and hot, sensual breath. Molten waves of desire coursed through her as she leaned even closer against him.

When he drew away, a shaft of coldness replaced his warmth. She inhaled deeply while he stepped away, bringing his own breathing under control.

"The timing isn't right, Rae. I want you, but when you're emotionally ready." His uneven voice sent her senses soaring.

"You're right," she murmured, then quickly slid behind the driver's seat and drove away.

Thank God he couldn't see the blush that covered her cheeks. She had discovered something tonight that shocked her, and yet intrigued her at the same time. She could have given herself to a man she barely knew to satisfy an emptiness that was screaming for fulfillment.

Jonathan rubbed the back of his neck as he watched Rae drive away. He knew she hadn't been ready for him. It was too soon after her father's death for her to be sure about her emotions. She had reached out for comfort in her time of grief. Would any human being have satisfied her need? In his heart he hoped not.

As Jonathan made his way back into the house, he heard a car approach. He glanced back and saw his sister slamming Bradley's door shut and stomping up the steps.

"My, you're home early," Jonathan teased, holding the front door open for her.

"And your date left early. Are you losing your touch, brother dear?"

"Didn't Bradley go along with one of your ideas?" He decided to let Carole's barb go unanswered. He was in a good mood. The evening had been successful and tomorrow promised to be even more interesting.

"No. He asked me to marry him and I told him I wasn't ready to settle down. He didn't like my answer. I think I'm going to leave for New York tomorrow."

"He'll only follow you, Carole. Bradley's a very single-minded man."

"Well, he's met his match in me," she huffed, storming toward the bar, where she fixed herself a brandy. "Can you imagine Bradley *telling* me he wanted me as his wife and mother of his children! I wouldn't mind having a child, but I'll decide when and with whom."

Jonathan's mouth quirked into a wide grin. "My, my, he doesn't know you very well . . . or does he?"

Carole nearly shattered the snifter as she brought it down hard on the bar. "No, he doesn't!" Her full mouth formed a pout as she brushed her long brown hair away from her face. "I don't want to talk about Bradley anymore. Let's discuss Rae Hamilton and Hamilton Oil. What are you planning, big brother?"

"No comment."

Carole planted her hands on her waist and glared at him. "I have a right to know. I own some shares in King Industries."

"But I control them until you're thirty or married."

"Then I might just marry Bradley after all."

Jonathan lifted his shoulders in a shrug. "It wouldn't make much difference. I'll still control the company and maybe Bradley could do something about you."

"You're exasperating, brother dear. Poor Rae. Maybe I should call her before I leave and warn her about what she's getting into."

Jonathan crossed the distance between them in three angry strides. He took Carole's upper arms in a tight grip and stared down at her with a menacing look. "If you do, you'll regret ever picking up the phone. What is or will be between Rae and myself is *our* business, not yours. Do I make myself clear?"

The coiled fury in Jonathan made Carole immediately realize her mistake. Unable to speak, she nodded her head, and he relinquished his bruising hold.

"I was only teasing, Jonathan," she said moments later as he moved to leave the living room. "But I can see there is much more than business between you and Rae."

Without a word Jonathan walked from the room. An image of a beautiful woman with hair that held touches of fire and eyes that shone like newly polished silver monopolized his thoughts. *No, not yet, Carole. But there will be soon.*

Chapter Three

$\mathcal{A}$ loud buzzing sound woke Rae up. She fumbled with the alarm and finally turned it off, then struggled out of bed. All the restless nights had caught up with her as she tried to shake off the drowsiness that still clung to her. Eight hours of sleep wasn't enough, her body screamed. Rae glanced back at her brass bed and wished she could stretch out again and sleep the day away.

Then the thought of her first staff meeting as president of Hamilton Oil galvanized her into action. After quickly showering and dressing, she grabbed a glass of orange juice and a piece of toast before heading for her car.

As Rae entered Hamilton Oil's office building and rode the elevator up to the second floor, she looked the perfect lady executive.

She was dressed in a tailored beige suit with a white silk blouse. The suit was conservative, something she thought was necessary for a woman in the business world. But the silk blouse with its simple lines had a certain softness to it that gave her outfit a feminine touch.

Rae crossed the reception room, nodding toward her father's secretary, now hers, as she opened the door to his office. Since her father's death, she had been in here just once, and as she stepped into the office, a feeling of isolation settled over her.

The massive oak desk where she had often found her father hard at work dominated the room, immediately catching her attention. "As a business associate enters your office, the focal point must be your desk and you." Her father's advice came to mind.

But he hadn't had time to teach her everything she needed to know. The risks—and the money—were great.

That's it, Rae Sinclair Hamilton! That's the last negative thought you will have, she told herself firmly. She could do anything she wanted to. She had overcome obstacles in the past and she would now.

Rae glanced at her watch and noted there were only thirty more minutes until she would meet with her department heads. Walking to the desk, Rae sat down and took several deep breaths before she opened her attaché case and began going over a prospect report on new land leases.

When her secretary knocked, Rae was so

absorbed that she nearly jumped out of her chair. Quickly her sense of bearing returned, and she looked up as Mrs. Daniels advanced into the room.

"Ordinarily I know you wouldn't want to be disturbed before the staff meeting. But Mr. Jonathan King is waiting to see you. He doesn't have an appointment, but your father—"

Rae waved her hand and said, "That's fine, Mrs. Daniels. I have a few minutes. Show Mr. King in and then buzz me when it's time for the staff meeting."

Rae's curiosity was aroused. Why was Jonathan here this morning? Again she relived his kiss in her mind. This morning, in the bright light of day with a good night's sleep, her defenses wouldn't vanish as easily as they had last evening. He had been right. She wasn't herself lately.

When Jonathan entered her office, he reminded Rae for an instant of a predator staking out his territory. This morning he wore a ruthless look she had often seen in her father's eyes when he went in for the kill. The planes of Jonathan's face seemed carved out of steel—hard, durable and unbending. Everything about him spelled danger.

"I see you got a good night's rest, Rae."

Even his voice was velvet-covered steel. She shuddered at the way Jonathan moved into her office, as though he owned the place. Her instincts told her to beware, to not let down her guard for one second.

Standing straight with her shoulders

squared and her chin lifted, Rae asked in a businesslike voice, "What can I do for you, Mr. King?"

"We have some business to discuss, *Miss Hamilton*. I suggest we sit and talk before your staff meeting." His voice was equally formal, almost curt.

"Which is in only fifteen minutes. Can't this wait until after the meeting? I pride myself on not being late."

"Well, for once you'll have to be." Jonathan sat in the chair in front of her desk and waited for her to sit down.

Something about him warned her to comply. Across the expanse of her desk they measured each other as if they were opponents, circling, waiting to make the first strike. Then the blow hit Rae like a sledgehammer.

"I'm buying the sixteen percent of Hamilton Oil that's needed for me to own the controlling interest," Jonathan said calmly, his eyes narrowing as he waited for her reaction. But there was none, not even a flicker of surprise or anger. *My God, this woman would be an excellent poker player!*

"And just how do you propose to do that?" she finally asked in a steady voice which didn't reflect her quivering rage.

The nerve of this man! Sixteen percent indeed! He doesn't even own one percent, or does he? Suddenly Rae recalled the grave financial trouble Hamilton Oil had been heading for two years ago. There had been talk of going public, something her father hadn't wanted to do. He had always wanted and fought hard for full control of the business.

Then all of a sudden things began to work out for the company. At the time she had been too busy taking over as the drilling manager to question her father in detail. She had accepted his word that everything was fine. Now, she wished she had insisted on the truth.

Jonathan opened his briefcase, withdrew some papers and slid them across the desk toward Rae. "Read for yourself. Then, when you understand, we'll talk business."

Rae carefully began to read the legal documents outlining the business partnership between her father and Jonathan King and the option Jonathan had if her father died before he could buy back Jonathan's shares. It took all her willpower to keep her shock hidden behind a calm facade. She wondered why her father hadn't told her. Why couldn't he have shared this with her? She was his only daughter and heir, and yet he had kept this a secret. Her heart burned with hurt and humiliation, but to Jonathan her expression remained neutral.

She was an incredible actress, Jonathan thought as he examined her brows knitting in concentration and her wintry-gray eyes sharpening. "Upset" would have been a mild word to describe his reaction if someone had walked into his office and said he would be buying controlling interest in King Industries.

The intercom's buzz cut into Rae's intense

study of the contracts. She flipped the switch, told her secretary to reschedule the staff meeting for two in the afternoon, and then returned to finish reading the last document.

Carefully—too carefully—she placed the papers in a neat pile before her, then looked up at Jonathan. She wanted to ask him so many questions. Why hadn't her father told anyone, especially her? Why did Jonathan want the sixteen percent? But she would wait and listen. Hadn't that been Jonathan's advice last night?

"According to this"—she flicked her hand toward the paper—"you can buy the necessary shares from my father's estate at fair market value if you choose to or you can retain your thirty-five percent until I can afford to buy back *all* your shares. The choice is *yours,* not mine."

She looked so prim and proper, so hard-sounding, that Jonathan couldn't resist saying, "You read quite well, Rae."

"If we are going to have any kind of business relationship, I would like you to please refrain from making statements like that in the future. You'll find I'm quite competent in my field and demand respect."

"You're right about being a good engineer, Rae, but as far as I'm concerned that's all I'll acknowledge. You have yet to prove to me that you can run this company successfully."

"Have you ever heard of giving someone a chance?" For a few seconds an emotion flickered in her eyes; then it was gone.

"Yes, but not with so much money at stake.

If everything went well, you still couldn't buy back my interest for at least another year and that's a long time when millions of dollars are involved. This company could run into a serious cash flow problem before I even realized it."

Rae stood and walked to the window, staring out with unseeing eyes. "Okay, so you're going to buy the controlling interest, then what? Are you going to run Hamilton Oil from your Dallas office? What are your intentions toward this company?" She turned to face him, tension thickening the air between them. "After all, I do have a right to know since I'll own the other forty-nine percent."

"My office can run smoothly without my presence every day." Jonathan rose and closed the distance between them. "I will commute between Tulsa and Dallas when necessary. Until I'm satisfied you can run this company, I'll make *all* the final decisions. In the meantime, I'll teach you about financial matters and managing a business."

"But—"

He held up his hand, his expression warning her not to protest. "Being an engineer, the head of only one department in Hamilton Oil, and running and overseeing all five departments are two entirely different jobs. I'm only going to complete the education that your father started."

She should be grateful, but she resented this man walking in here and taking what she considered hers—Hamilton Oil. And worse yet, he had known what he was going to do last night when he invited her to dinner—and kissed her later.

"And after that?" She was barely able to contain her anger now as she stepped back to place more distance between them. The office was becoming incredibly hot and stifling.

"If you live up to my standards, then you may take over Hamilton Oil's management until you can afford to buy back my shares. I don't have to honor your father's wish to leave the company in the family now that he's dead, but I will."

"Oh, how kind of you."

The distance between them vanished rapidly as Jonathan faced her with only inches separating them. "That decision can be changed at any time. I have been known to be very ruthless and unbending in my business dealings, but right now I think I have enough companies that I don't feel I have to add Hamilton Oil to the list. That can change, though, Miss Hamilton, so watch your step."

The chilling calm in his words sent a shiver down her spine. "So you hold all the cards, and there's nothing I can do to change your mind about buying the shares."

"You could try, but if I were you, I would save my energy and learn the business quickly. However, if you want to take your time, that's okay with me, too." Desire gleamed in his eyes for a brief moment.

Rae looked him squarely in the eye and said in a frosting tone, "If you would please leave my office . . . I must contact my father's lawyer and see to some details." Mr. Davis had wanted to read the will the week before, but she had been so busy that she had asked to wait until this week. Now, she wished she had made the time. It wouldn't have changed the situation, but it would have been better if she had known about this sooner—before last night.

One of Jonathan's eyebrows rose mockingly. "*Your* office?"

"Oh, I see, Mr. King. First you take my company from me, then you try to take something much more personal, and now you also want my father's office."

With an amused look on his face, he asked, "Where would you suggest, Miss Hamilton, that I set up my office?"

"Dallas."

Laughter rumbled deep in his chest. "You won't be able to get rid of me that easily."

Exasperated, Rae moved back to her desk and sat behind it, as though to assert her claim to rightfully occupy the chair. "This is *my* office. Fend for yourself, Mr. King. I'm sure you're quite good at that."

"If I wasn't in such a good mood, I would take you up on that challenge. As it is, I've already arranged for the office next door to be mine."

"But that's where the staff meets."

"It will be my office. The staff will have to meet somewhere else. You're smart. Think of a place. Now, I'll leave you to your thoughts and be back in two hours to take you to lunch."

"No, thank you. I may be forced to work

with you, but I don't care to ruin my lunch, too." Rae was clenching the arms of her chair so tightly that her fingertips were turning red.

"Have you ever heard of a *business* lunch, Miss Hamilton? We still have a few things to discuss before the staff meeting—like what to tell *our* department heads."

She wanted to say, "It's your company now. You tell them anything you please." Wasn't that what he would do anyway?

But Rae turned her thoughts away from the turbulent ground they were heading for and toward calmer, more rational thoughts. "Then I'll see you in two hours, Mr. King," she finally said before returning her attention to the report on land leases.

When she heard the door shut, she looked up at the space where Jonathan had been standing. What a mess! How could her father have sold part of the company without her knowledge, and to such an impossible man at that? Would she ever satisfy Jonathan King? Would he decide in a year or so not to sell her his half of the company? Nothing bound him to what he had said today. She was at his mercy. These next months were going to be the longest ones of her life!

After placing a call to her father's lawyer, who confirmed everything, she slowly forced her attention back to business. She'd made an appointment to see Mr. Davis tomorrow morning. With that taken care of, she went over the reports from each department head. Several times she found herself rereading a page a second time because her thoughts strayed to Jonathan. Her new boss. Bitterness overwhelmed her at the thought. She might not know a lot about business administration and finances, but did he know about the oil industry? Today at lunch she had every intention of finding out just how much Jonathan King knew.

Later, seated across from him at a restaurant, Rae again found her anger simmering below her composed front. He had marched into her office unannounced exactly two hours later to take her to lunch. She had had to drop what she had been in the middle of doing to comply with his majesty's wish. Smiling, she recalled that she had literally dropped the paper she had been reading when he had barged into her office without warning. He did have a way of overpowering a person, she decided.

"I'm glad to see you're accepting the situation so graciously," Jonathan said.

"I don't really have any choice, do I? Mr. Davis confirmed the deal, so I'm stuck with you," Rae replied nonchalantly, her smile fading.

"Does anything ever get under your skin?"

"Why do you ask? Do you want to see me blow up? What would that accomplish, Mr. King?" *If Jonathan only knew*, Rae thought, *that I would like to have told him to go to the devil about a dozen times already today.*

Since the waiter appeared to take their orders, Jonathan refrained from answering. But after the waiter had left, he said, "You're definitely a woman of contradictions. A woman with such flaming hair should have a temper to match, but instead I discover a Nordic ice queen under that fiery exterior. Doesn't it ever get lonely in that ivory tower of yours?"

With a piercing look which came close to revealing her anger, she ignored his question and said, "In the business world, losing your temper only makes matters worse, especially for a woman. If I had shouted at the men in the field, they probably would have laughed in my face and written me off as some hysterical, irrational woman who happened to be the boss's daughter trying to prove herself in a man's profession." Her voice was low, none of the frustrations she had experienced over the years evident.

"So you learned to bury any feelings you might have. Have you made the walls so high that they're impossible to climb, Rae?"

"That, sir, is none of your business, and I might add never will be. Since we're here for business reasons, I suggest we discuss business."

Rae took several sips of her cold water to extinguish the angry flame which threatened to explode into a raging inferno if Jonathan continued to press her.

"Of course, Rae. We only have another hour until you present me to our staff."

Why did he have to keep saying "our"? It made everything sound so personal. Again

Rae sipped her cold water, until she had drained the glass. Then she finally asked, "And how do you want me to introduce you, Mr. King?"

"First, I insist on your using my given name. After all, we are partners now."

There he goes again, making this situation sound intimate, Rae thought. "*Business* partners," she informed him.

"Second, I think the best way would be the truth—at least part of it. I think we should tell them that we're partners and will run the company jointly. Of course, the whole truth will be that I have final word on all the big decisions. The staff doesn't need to know that. Let them think we present a united front. They're used to you and your father and it will be an easier transition if handled this way. Also, if you do meet my standards, it will be easier for you to take over completely later on if it appears that you have been in charge all along."

"You're so thoughtful." Rae said sweetly, but there was venom beneath the soft words.

"Well, it's about time you saw one of my finer points."

"What do you know about the oil industry, Mr. King?"

"I wondered when you would ask."

The laughter in his voice made Rae seethe. "I do have a right to ask. I need to know where you're coming from."

"I have quite a lot of investments in different programs with various oil companies."

"Investing in programs is one thing and knowing how, when and where to drill is another."

His smile wavered. His hard expression conveyed to Rae that not many people questioned his expertise.

"Rae, if you had checked into my background, you would have found out that I also own Fraser Oil. I'm a lawyer and I've worked extensively in the real estate end of the industry as a landman. That's how I made most of my money. Now, though, oil is only a part of my corporation's interest."

"What's to stop you from taking the information at Hamilton and using it for Fraser?" Her anger finally surfaced, appearing in the hardened look in her eyes, the clamped jaws, the rigid body. "Or to merge the two companies?"

"Because Fraser operates mainly in Texas and Louisiana, while Hamilton is based in Oklahoma. It's to my benefit financially for them to remain separate. Now, I'll admit I'm not an engineer or geologist, but I do know about the oil industry from a financial standpoint. Satisfied?"

"No, I'm not satisfied with the situation, but then my opinion doesn't matter."

"It could if you play your cards right." Mischief etched a wide grin into his features.

Rae was gritting her teeth so hard that her jaw began to ache. Everything was falling apart. Her well-ordered life was being turned upside down by one man.

"Relax, Rae. I'm not the big bad wolf you

think I am. When I give my word, I keep it. When you get to know me better, you'll realize that. Your father did."

"Maybe my father wasn't as shrewd a businessman as I thought." Brittle tension blanketed her in a cold fury.

"Ah, I see our meal has arrived. Enjoy it, then we'd better leave for the meeting."

Enjoy the lunch! How could she when inside her stomach was tied in a hundred tiny knots? Rae picked at her food and finally gave up trying to eat and finished her coffee.

At the end of the meal, Jonathan leaned back, placed his napkin on the table, and said in a smug voice, "Mmm. That was a delicious steak. Are you ill? You didn't touch your shrimp and it looks so good."

"Do you want to eat my meal, too?" she asked sarcastically.

"No, we don't have the time," he answered pleasantly, ignoring her taunt.

Jonathan paid the bill, then escorted her to his coupe. Why couldn't he have a large Lincoln, instead of this small sports car which subjected her to his disturbing closeness? His distinctive male scent drifted to her nostrils, vividly reminding her of the night before. Anger and embarrassment stained her cheeks red. In that instant she realized it would be difficult to resist him if she let her emotions rule her.

Even now in the small confines of his Mercedes, her body was reacting traitorously. A weakness was spreading through her, and when Jonathan shifted and accidentally touched her leg, her heart began to race. It was as though there were two Raes, one manipulated by her mind and another by her body. By the time they reached the office she knew she would have to keep her distance until common sense had prevailed.

With her heated emotions subdued, Rae entered the large office that had quickly been made into the new staff meeting room. Questioning stares from her department heads greeted her entrance, but each manager kept silent, allowing her a chance to further gather her thoughts into a plan of action.

Rae stood coolly at the head of the long table and scanned each man's face once before she launched into her speech, thanking them for their support and hoping for their continued excellent work. Then, after pausing for a few seconds, Rae turned and met Jonathan's gaze.

"Gentlemen, I know you've all been speculating about the activities that have been occurring this morning and I think it's time I explain." Rae was in complete command now as she continued. "Mr. King was my father's silent partner, and upon his death has now become my partner. We will both jointly run Hamilton Oil." She almost choked on the last sentence. Lying went against all she stood for, and yet she understood it was for the best that someone familiar to the company employees seem to be in charge.

Slowly the shock at the announcement faded and only doubt and questions remained.

Rae could tell some of the men had heard of Jonathan King. Their expressions turned from awe to suspicion. No doubt these men also knew about Fraser Oil and wondered what Jonathan was up to. They were all asking themselves, *Why is Jonathan King no longer remaining a silent partner?*

Jonathan stood and addressed the department heads. "I'll be working with Miss Hamilton, and in the next week I would like to meet with each one of you to go over your departments."

Everyone was prepared for a long speech and was surprised when Jonathan sat down. For a full minute silence thickened the already heavy air. All eyes turned to her, and Rae glanced over her agenda, again feeling unsure of herself. She felt as though she were on stage giving a speech in front of a hundred hostile people, when in actuality there was only one—Jonathan King.

"Hamilton Oil has at the moment three hundred wells in production, six being drilled, and nine pending. We have ninety thousand acres in land leases that we haven't acted on, with leases on ten thousand acres coming up for renewal in the next few months . . ."

Jonathan reclined with his elbows on the chair's arms, his fingers forming a steeple. When Rae spoke, there was a quality of authority behind her words that he liked. She would need it if she were going to manage Hamilton Oil successfully. He listened to her review where Hamilton Oil stood and what needed to be done in the next few weeks, and his admiration heightened. She had certainly done her homework. She might be an engineer, but she was definitely showing him this afternoon that she knew Hamilton Oil's situation.

When the meeting ended an hour later, the individual managers waited to introduce themselves personally to Jonathan.

George Mason, the head geologist, hung back from the group clustered around Mr. King and observed quietly, something he was very good at doing. Rae was aggravated about something. Not many people could read it in her aloof, professional expression, but he had known her all her life and recognized the little signs that indicated her anger—a certain hard look, a slight tensing around the mouth.

George knew that several years back Hamilton Oil had been in trouble, but lately it had been doing better. In fact, if his latest study proved what he thought, the company would make a bundle on the newest venture he would soon propose to Rae.

Now, looking closely at Rae, George decided that something was going on here that he wasn't being told. Even if Raymond had sold part of the company, he wouldn't have given up control. Why were Rae and Mr. King now running it *jointly*? George asked himself again. She loved the company as much as her father had and George couldn't see her willingly sharing the control. There was too much of her father in her.

"George Mason, I would like you to meet Jonathan King," Rae said, drawing the geologist into the cluster.

George shook Jonathan's hand, sizing the younger man up. Jonathan King had built up his father's small, Tulsa-based company until he now ran a large conglomerate with many companies the size of his father's under his control. He was a respected businessman, admired by many for his Midas touch, feared by others for his killer instinct, which he could use when necessary.

George said a few polite words to Mr. King, then stepped aside as Rae introduced Shane Travis. George had been with Hamilton Oil for over twenty-five years, since the company had been founded. He had seen many things and been through a lot of ups and downs. He resolved to have a talk with Rae. He owed it to her father, a longtime friend.

After introducing the department heads, Rae moved away from Jonathan. Suddenly weary, she sought to escape. George caught up with her when she reached for the doorknob.

"May I have a word with you, Rae?"

Stepping out into the corridor, she smiled faintly at the geologist. "Let's go into my office, George. I went over your report yesterday on that field. It looks good."

"I've had my share of wrong guesses, but in my bones I feel there's a lot of oil and gas down there. Of course, you can't go on what my bones say, but my study of the subsurface map indicates it, too." He grinned as he opened the door to Rae's office and allowed her to enter ahead of him.

"What do you think we'll have to pay for the mineral rights?"

"There aren't any wells in the area, so the land ought to be cheap. Say three hundred dollars an acre."

"Good. I'll get back to you on it." Rae had wanted to say, "Go ahead," but now she had to check out everything with Jonathan. It goaded her to have to, but she had no choice until she knew from Jonathan what she could or couldn't do. She saw the puzzled look on George's face and knew he was wondering why she was waiting.

"Rae, what's the deal with Mr. King?"

If anyone else had asked her that, she would have given him a chilling look, then told him to mind his own business. But George was different. George, Carl and her father had been a three-man team at the beginning of Hamilton Oil, and she couldn't ignore that fact. Obviously her father had told no one about the partnership, and she was beginning to understand why. Her father had hated to admit any failure, and to openly acknowledge Hamilton Oil was in financial trouble would have been admitting failure—a big one, since the company was his whole life. She would respect her father's wishes and remain quiet.

"It's just like I said. Mr. King and I are partners." She would tell him no more.

"Okay, Rae. I can read between the lines. Mind my own business. Let me know about the property soon. And don't forget the group of investors from New York who are arriving at the end of next week. I hope they buy the program your father developed. It's a good one."

The door between her office and Jonathan's opened, halting George's progress toward the outer door. Unannounced again, Jonathan stepped into Rae's office, knowing full well she hadn't been alone.

Quickly assessing the situation, Jonathan advanced into the room, saying, "You're just the man I've been looking for, George. I would like to have a word with you later this afternoon. Would four-thirty be convenient?" It wasn't really a question but an order.

"Fine."

"I want to familiarize myself with the investment program before those people from New York arrive and I have some ideas for a new program. I'll be gone the rest of the week, so I'll need to look it over this evening."

It didn't take Jonathan long, Rae thought. She wouldn't be surprised if he knew where every well was, how much it was producing, the taxes the company paid on it, and where their land leases were—in short, everything there was to know.

When George left, Rae turned to Jonathan, her eyes showing her annoyance. "You may be the senior partner in this—partnership, but I won't have you come barging into *my* office unannounced. What did you expect to find?" Her leashed temper finally burst from its tight restraints. "I will *not* tolerate that from you.

I'm entitled to some privacy and your respect. You cannot bulldoze me. *If* you keep your word, in a year *or less* I'll be the sole owner of Hamilton Oil and I must retain my staff's respect. So don't undermine me!" Fury turned her gray eyes as dark as the clouds in an approaching thunderstorm.

He merely smiled at her, as if her words had been honey-coated instead of poison-filled. He was impossible! She had never felt so much anger toward another human being and she couldn't seem to contain it anymore.

"My, my, so you do have a temper after all. I was beginning to think you had ice in your veins," Jonathan said, his smile dissolving under the blaze in her eyes. "You'll find, Rae, that I do little I don't want to. If you want my respect, you'll have to earn every minute bit of it. I don't give it easily, as you'll find out." His deadly quiet voice frosted her with its frigid calm.

"If you have nothing else to discuss with me, then please leave *my* office." Every muscle was taut as she stood with her arms stiff at her sides.

"I came in here to tell you that there will be a dinner party at my house next Thursday night for the New York investors. You'll act as my hostess. Then on Friday we'll take them out to one of our fields before we have our business meeting."

"Why do you even bother saying 'our'? Don't you really mean *yours* now? You have effectively come in and taken over even if you didn't make a broadcast to the whole staff. Do you think they're blind? I had to tell George I would get back to him on a land deal because I have to get *your* okay. I should have been able to say yes right then and there, and George knew it. I don't even know when I'm allowed to make a decision or when I have to refer it to you."

"I'll take a look at it and let you know before I leave for Dallas tomorrow afternoon."

"What do I do while you're gone? Twiddle my thumbs?"

Jonathan moved until he stood only inches from her. "Have you ever heard of the telephone, Miss Hamilton?" His voice knifed through her with its icy splinters. "The routine matters you can take care of, but if something important comes up in the few days I'm gone, call. I promise you the phone is quite an effective little machine."

"And what do you call routine? Buying land leases is pretty routine to me."

"Use your judgment. If it's anything involving a lot of money, I want to okay it first. As you prove yourself, you'll have more of an input into the final decisions."

Her eyes widened in mock surprise. "You're going to leave something up to me!"

His hands shot up to frame her face. She could only interpret the smoldering glow in his dark eyes as fury, and she tried to free herself. The tension between them threatened to snap. He held her pinned beneath his contemptuous gaze, but she challenged his anger with an unshakable resolve.

"I am basically a fairly patient man, but you

are doing your damnedest to stretch my patience to its limit, Rae Hamilton. We are partners for at least the next year whether you like it or not." Jonathan released her and strode toward the connecting door between their offices.

Rae thought about having the door walled in but knew it would be useless. Jonathan would only have it torn down, if that was what he wanted.

On the second ring of the bell, Rae answered the door, belting her robe securely about her waist. Lounging against the wooden rail of the front porch was Jonathan King, still dressed in the three-piece gray suit he had worn earlier when he had told her he would be running Hamilton Oil.

"And to what do I owe the pleasure of seeing you again so soon?" She looked pointedly at her watch and added sarcastically, "After business hours."

"Luck." Jonathan walked into her apartment and sat down on her couch, making himself right at home.

"Please take off your coat and tie—and your shoes, of course. Make yourself comfortable, by all means." A biting edge had crept into her voice as she stood by the still-opened door.

"Close the door and let's talk, Rae."

"As far as I'm concerned we did all our talking earlier at the office. You're on *my* time now, Mr. King, and I want you to leave." Rae opened the door even wider.

"I have to leave later tonight instead of

tomorrow afternoon, so we need to go over some things. And frankly, I don't want the neighbors to hear about Hamilton Oil's business."

"You could have used the telephone and called me. You know, someone recently told me the phone is quite an effective little machine. You should try it sometime."

"Ouch. That barb struck its mark."

His infuriatingly enchanting smile took the fight out of her. It had been a *very* long day. Slowly she closed the door, using that time to marshal her defenses against Jonathan.

"Since I have to be at the airport in an hour, let's get down to business. I had hoped to have a little more time before going back to Dallas to wrap up some loose ends there."

"It's a shame you don't. Please stay away an extra week. Don't rush back on my account."

"Not on your account but on Hamilton Oil's account."

"Bull's-eye. Touché."

An unwilling smile graced her features. Dull and boring would never be two words to associate with Jonathan King. She resented his intrusion into her life, but there was a sense of excitement about him that made her wish she had met him under different circumstances.

Don't kid yourself. You wouldn't have allowed yourself the time to get to know him better, Rae Hamilton. You're too involved with Hamilton Oil.

"First, have George buy that land, but go no higher than four hundred dollars an acre. It may be everything he feels. It certainly looks promising. Second, by the time I return to Tulsa I would like a detailed report on all of Hamilton's existing wells. You know all the information that's pertinent. Third, I want you and George to start putting in time developing that new investment program I discussed with him today. I would like it to be the largest program Hamilton Oil has ever offered."

"And just where are you going to get the extra investors for this new program of yours? Out of your hat?"

Jonathan stood and lessened the space between them in three quick steps. "You forget my expertise is finance. You and George work up a good program and I'll sell it."

"Somehow I have no doubt you will."

Their gazes collided and locked.

"I'm glad you think I have some usefulness."

"What I think means nothing, Mr. King."

"Jonathan. We are partners, after all."

"Not by choice."

Jonathan cupped her face in his hands, their gazes still bound, as if some invisible force were dictating their actions. One of his hands slid around to pull her head toward his, his lips claiming hers. The raw urgency of his kiss rendered her limp and suddenly vulnerable. She could fight anything but this wildly exciting desire he ignited in her.

Her thoughts centered on sensations: the rich thickness of his hair as her fingers combed through it; the slight roughness of his jaw; the soothing massage of his hands now drawing her closer against him. She was experiencing something entirely alien—a primitive need to be close to Jonathan.

When his mouth moved slowly to her earlobe, the devastating risk in his embrace dazed her mind.

"Isn't this better than fighting, Rae?"

His husky question brought her common sense back in full force, and she pulled away.

"No, it isn't! This is a *business* partnership and nothing else. I hope you'll have the decency to remember that in the future, Mr. King."

"Whoever said I was decent?" There was a laughing wickedness in his eyes as he headed for the front door. "I'll see you in a few days." Then he was gone.

Rae sank into a chair, the trembling starting in her hands and spreading rapidly throughout her. If she didn't pull herself together, she would be lost.

She had seen the desire in his eyes, the naked lust for her. He did nothing to conceal it. It was as though he wanted her to know his intentions and to have her prepare for the inevitable. Conflicting sensations confused her; she was both excited and frightened.

Chapter Four

It was midafternoon, but Rae's eyes burned as if she had been up reading all night and dawn was breaking on the horizon. Looking toward the bright sunlight flooding through the one large picture window in her office, she dropped her pen and stood, stretching. Her muscles were cramped from hours sitting at her desk working on the new program Hamilton Oil would soon be offering their investors. The remains of a half-eaten sandwich and a cold cup of coffee sat on her desk.

Her gaze shifted to the coffee, its dark color instantly reminding her of Jonathan's eyes. He was the reason she was pushing herself to work fifteen hours a day. She vowed she soon would know more than he did on how to run Hamilton Oil. She wanted that man out of her life and if that meant slaving away even *eighteen* hours a day she would gladly do it—anything to get him to sell her his shares when she raised the necessary money.

In the eleven days since he had declared he owned fifty-one percent of Hamilton Oil, her world had completely changed. There was nothing stable in her life anymore—not even her job. She had counted on the company being the one steadying influence after her father's death, and Jonathan had taken that away from her. He sat in the office next to hers and directed *her* employees, as though he had been there for years. Even though they appeared to be equal partners to the staff, Rae had found many of the male department heads seeking Jonathan's advice or opinion, and these were people she had been working with for years. She felt betrayed—and yes, jealous—of Jonathan's natural leadership ability. People automatically sought him out and valued what he said. It wasn't fair!

The intercom buzzed and Rae pressed the button. "Yes, Mrs. Daniels?"

"Mr. Travis is here for your meeting."

"Send him in, please."

Rae straightened, smoothed her hair and skirt into place, then walked across the spacious office to meet Shane as he entered. Offering him a bright smile, she asked, "How do you like being the drilling manager?"

A grin spread over his whole face, handsome in a classical sort of way, and his hazel eyes twinkled. "The extra money is appreciated, ma'am."

Rae tucked her arm through his and led him toward the couch. With Shane having started as an engineer at Hamilton Oil six months after her, they had been friends for years. He was good, and Rae felt lucky that the company had his services.

"I'm sorry I've been so busy that we haven't had time to talk more," Rae said as they sat next to each other on the couch.

"You don't have to apologize, Rae. You only lost your father three weeks ago and now this situation with Mr. King . . ." He left his sentence unfinished, as if the silence said it all.

Realizing Shane was one of the few people on the staff who held back where Jonathan was concerned, Rae asked, "What do you think of my business—associate?" She couldn't bring herself to say "partner." That still sounded too personal and intimate to her.

"I'm not sure. You know, Rae, that sometimes engineers and management don't always see eye to eye on how to run the company, especially the rigs."

"I know. Even my father and I had our arguments, but basically he agreed with my approach."

"Well, I thought it would be different when you ran the company. Rae, why is Hamilton Oil continuing to drill on number two Jones? I recommended we stop at twelve thousand feet. But the directive I received from your office is that we continue to thirteen thousand. I know there's good reason to suspect there's gas between twelve and thirteen thousand, but the risks are high. You know what the mud weight is and that we can't increase the weight without risky well control. I know some companies take the risks and drill further, but Hamilton has always been more conservative."

Shane didn't have to explain. She remembered recommending on Monday to halt drilling, but Jonathan had the final say. And obviously he had ignored Shane's and her recommendations and was doing what he pleased! Rae felt caught in the middle. She heartily agreed with Shane, but then she was an engineer and knew very well the grave risks involved.

"Rae, if there's a blowout, it will be costly to Hamilton. There's some gas above ten thousand. Let's take that and get out. Our policy in the past—"

Stiffly Rae rose, a frown creasing her brow. "Thank you, Shane, for your concern. This isn't only my decision but Mr. King's, too."

"I knew it! This didn't sound like something you would do. You're more cautious and this is definitely not a conservative move."

"I hope you're coming to the dinner tonight at Mr. King's," she said, dismissing the subject of number two Jones and making it clear by her expression it was useless to question her further.

"It's a command performance. I couldn't miss it," Shane said jokingly. "Secretly I've always wondered what his huge, old mansion off Utica looked like inside and this is my chance."

"Then I'll see you tonight at seven-thirty."

Rae directed Shane toward the door, and the second he left her office she drew in a deep breath and walked purposefully toward Jonathan's door. Without knocking she stepped into his private domain.

Jonathan was so absorbed in a report that he didn't hear Rae enter. She studied the intense concentration on his face, the powerful hands that held the paper. Her gaze took in the arrogant nose, the cleft in his strong chin, and his mouth which seemed hard in repose.

Looking up finally, Jonathan caught her bold appraisal, an odd expression drifting across his face before it settled into an unreadable mask.

"And to what do I owe this—interruption?" Jonathan laid the report on the desk, sensing the ensuing battle, and squared his shoulders as if readying himself for the conflict.

"How could you do it to me?" There was none of Rae's usual dispassionate tone in the question. Her voice quavered slightly with her anger.

His lips quirked before curving into an amused grin. It looked as if he were loving every minute of her anger!

"Do what, Rae?" he drawled in a maddeningly patient voice.

Standing in the doorway that connected their offices, Rae was like a time bomb, methodically ticking away. She desperately tried to still the raging fury that sped to every nerve ending, striking against each one like flint. She needed more than anything at this moment to approach Jonathan thoroughly in control and completely composed. But staring at his infuriatingly smug smile made the blood pound in her temples and her desperate wish was ignored by the anger that made her tremble.

Jonathan knew he had penetrated her tough armor. Her gritted teeth indicated she was placing a restraint on her temper only with the greatest of difficulty, and this pleased him. She was feeling and showing something toward him. Even anger was better than the cool, bland poise of last week.

"You know perfectly well what I'm talking about, Mr. King." She *had* to keep this—discussion—on a very formal, businesslike level.

"I have many talents, *Rae*, but mind reading is not one of them. Would you care to enlighten me as to what has so beautifully ruffled your feathers?"

Her nerves quivered like plucked violin strings, and with an incredible effort she fought back a nasty retort. He was laughing at her! To him, she and Hamilton Oil must be only an amusing diversion. She could only hope that he would give up this game he was playing with her and her company and move on soon—*very soon*. She didn't know if she could take much more of this arrogant, pigheaded, opinionated, male chauvinistic man!

"Number two Jones. You have no business ordering the drilling to go past twelve thousand feet. We're on a fine line. We have just enough mud weight to control the pressure we've encountered so far. If we hit any more pressure, we may not be able to handle it. We risk losing well control and having a blow-out."

"Miss Hamilton! I'm very aware of what can happen to the well. Contrary to what you think I don't need a simple engineering lesson."

Fire sizzled through her at his condescending tone. "And I disagree. You need more than a simple engineering lesson. You should take a four-year course."

She became keenly aware of the chilling hostility which condensed the air like a menacing fog, making each step she took dangerous.

"I read your report as well as Shane Travis's, but financially it's a good move to go after the gas in this pay sand."

"Four Star has an offset to us and they hit too much pressure in that sand," she pointed out sarcastically.

"That is a calculated risk I'm willing to take."

"But I'm not."

They now stood only a foot apart, each taut, their gazes blazing.

"Must I constantly remind you that I make the final decisions, Rae? And this one stands. We'll continue to drill. That's final!"

His hot breath fanned her cheeks while his eyes bored into her. He wasn't used to having his authority questioned, and it seemed every time he turned around Rae Hamilton was doubting his judgment. She could get under a man's skin with one wintry look—or one brief smile which radiated a warmth she usually kept locked up inside, as if she wore a chastity belt to protect the true Rae Hamilton from the world. He swore by all he cared about that he would find the blasted key to unlock the mysteries of one Rae Hamilton.

"And I thought you were a good businessman, Mr. King."

His laughter filled the tension-laden air. "You mean you thought there was something good about me?"

"Correct. *Thought* is the key word." She backed away from him until she was pressed against the door. Fumbling for the knob, she said, "When the well blows, I'm going to take immense pleasure in saying I told you so. It's almost worth the money this company will lose. Almost, but not quite."

"And when the well strikes a lot of gas, my immense pleasure won't come from words, Rae."

The caressing quality of his voice propelled her to open the door and escape the frankly appreciative look in his midnight-dark eyes. Her cheeks burned from anger, she told herself fiercely. But in her heart she couldn't forget the naked desire which had flared to life when his eyes had raked over her one final time before she had fled.

The rest of the afternoon crawled slowly by. It was useless to try and kid herself into thinking she accomplished any constructive work. By four-thirty she had had enough of sitting at her desk staring at the papers before her and not really seeing any of the words. She was too incensed to think straight. The nerve of that man was colossal!

Rae left early. A few eyebrows rose at the time. She hadn't left before nine in the last two weeks. But she would need some time to collect herself before going to dinner at his home.

For weeks now she hadn't allowed herself many luxuries, but the first thing she did when she arrived at her apartment was to fill her tub with some bubble bath, then strip out of her clothes and enjoy the soothing effect of the hot water. It was the balm she needed to restore her nerves and give her strength to face the evening ahead.

Rae took her time selecting the right gown for the dinner. In the end she picked a simple black silk gown which flared at the waist and fell in soft folds about her long, slender legs. The bodice was a halter which left her back almost completely bare. When she surveyed herself in the mirror, she started to take it off. The gown was too seductive for a business dinner.

Then suddenly an impish gleam touched her eyes. Why not? The angry, bold approach hadn't worked. Maybe if she used her womanly wiles, she could get Jonathan to change his mind about number two Jones. She was becoming desperate where he was concerned.

With her confidence bolstered by the very feminine dress with its simple but alluring lines, Rae arrived at Jonathan's at precisely seven-thirty. When Jonathan opened the door instead of his butler, her surprise must have shown in her eyes.

One eyebrow lifted as he said, "The grandfather clock just chimed seven-thirty. I knew it would be you, so I relieved Samuel of his duty."

Since vinegar hasn't worked, try honey to get what you want, she told herself while moving into the foyer and allowing him to take her black lace shawl.

As she turned to face him with a smile, she heard his quick intake of breath and for the first time felt a power over this man. The raw sexuality he exuded was an almost tangible force which reached out and captured her in its overwhelming intensity. In the instant his desire was communicated, she also recognized the power he held over her. When he moved to draw her into his embrace, she was aware of the compelling danger and stepped quickly away.

"Are the guests here?" she asked. Was that her voice shaking?

"Right now I'm sorry to say yes. In the living room."

He didn't try to hold her. She had withdrawn, but he sensed her fluctuating like a barometer in unsteady weather conditions. However, he did move to stand in front of her, running his finger lightly down her bare arm.

That touch was weakening her firm control and she couldn't fight it. Darts of liquid heat quivered up her arm where his fingers had teased her skin, and the fire quickly consumed every inch of her body. Oh, God, this helpless feeling was too much to bear. She reached deep within for an unyielding resolve to combat her traitorous body before it was too late and she walked up the stairs to wait for him to get rid of the guests—*Hamilton's investors!*

Finally the sound of men's voices penetrated the haze of desire which had wrapped around her, and she jerked away from his sensual assault.

"Am I the last to arrive?" Her voice was evener now.

"No. Shane and George haven't arrived yet."

Rae attempted a smile which couldn't quite stay on her lips. They tingled from his passionate look, which was working to sabotage her newfound strength. When the doorbell rang, Rae took that opportunity to walk into the living room before Jonathan again assaulted her with his undivided attention.

What is happening to me? She couldn't believe how mixed up and confused she was becoming.

Glancing at the looks she received as she entered the room, the only female, she began to question wearing the alluring gown. It was so unlike her that she almost laughed aloud at the surprised looks on Shane's and George's faces when they entered the room. They knew her well and probably would not have recognized her if she hadn't been the only woman in a room full of men, their gazes trained on her in male interest, Jonathan's most of all.

Rae quickly began to mingle among the investors, whom she had known from other business transactions. All but one had invested with Hamilton Oil previously, and they were probably as surprised as George and Shane at her appearance. But before long they all realized she was still the professional businesswoman she had always been, and the atmosphere became more relaxed. Rae even found herself relaxing and enjoying the conversation until she was left alone by the bar, everyone else moving toward the dining room.

Jonathan held his arm out for her, a smile on his face, but underneath his smile lurked a tenseness that Rae felt when she hooked her arm through his. Her relaxed poise deserted her and she would have liked nothing better than to leave.

She began to pull her arm from his, but he tightened his hold painfully. "Smile, Rae. Remember, we must present a united front to our investors." Then, as he was seating her, he whispered close to her ear, "Which I hope will continue after they leave."

Rae mustered a semblance of a smile but didn't direct it at Jonathan. How could her father have ever considered this man as a partner? Then she had to laugh to herself. *Partner!* Jonathan didn't know the meaning of the word. He loved to dominate everyone around him, but he wouldn't succeed with her. He was wrong about number two Jones, and it was her duty to the company, *her* company, to make him see it.

The dinner passed uneventfully, if not successfully, as Rae read the mood of the investors afterward. Hamilton Oil would have no trouble obtaining the money it needed for the program. She had watched carefully while Jonathan had discussed the investment program her father had put together right before his death. It was a small program, nothing like what Jonathan proposed as their next venture, the one George, Jonathan and she were developing now. That program was just another example of the changes taking place at Hamilton Oil lately, all out of her control.

But no doubt Jonathan would find the investors for the new program they were working on. She had decided that Jonathan could persuade a mother to give up her child if he wanted to. He had a rare gift of perfect timing combined with charismatic appeal, which made it hard for anyone to deny his logic. Against her will she was impressed with his performance and she acknowledged to herself it was a performance.

After dinner Shane cornered her in the living room. "Has the status of number two Jones been changed?"

"No," she answered simply, adding no explanation.

She didn't like Shane reminding her that she had to sit back and watch someone else run her company, because as far as she was concerned, Hamilton Oil would always be hers. She didn't trust Jonathan's motives, a lesson her father had taught her well. "Don't give your trust easily, Rae," her father had told her on several occasions. "Most of the time people will let you down."

But Rae couldn't do anything to alter the situation. A piece of paper, however, couldn't change how she felt toward a fact she had grown up with and been groomed to accept most of her life. She had paid her dues. At a very young age she had changed and molded herself into someone her father would be proud of, someone her father thought capable of running an oil company. So why wouldn't Jonathan let her?

When the evening drew to an end Jonathan stood next to her, his arm about her waist effectively stopping her from leaving without causing a scene. It was as if they were more than partners. She thought it best to wait until everyone had left, then voice her objections to his overbearing tactics. With Jonathan, though, half the time she felt as if she were playing out of her league.

When the door closed on the last guest, Jonathan turned her to him, a smile gentling the hard planes of his face. "Okay. I'll listen for *one minute* to your dressing down. I can tell you're itching to give me one."

Rae fought the urge to return his smile. It was contagious. "Oh, I couldn't even begin to tell you off in that short a time. My grievance list is endless, Mr. King."

Silence hung heavily between them as they looked deeply into each other's eyes, each trying to read behind the other's mask. With his gaze never leaving her face, Jonathan moved his arms slowly about her, watching intently for any reaction.

"Do you know what you're doing to me, Rae?"

She nodded, hypnotized by the smoldering passion that flamed in his eyes.

His mouth descended slowly toward hers, giving her time to free herself from his embrace. But her legs wouldn't obey the order to move. Fascinated, she remained rooted to the floor and met the tender demand of his kiss with acceptance, yielding to his heated challenge.

His hands slid up her bare back, one slipping under her curtain of auburn hair to mold her head even closer. The sheer intensity of his throbbing desire silenced any resistance the sensible part of her was trying to muster.

For once it was wonderful just to feel, not to think rationally or worry about what would happen later. Right now, the present was all that mattered. The needs, the loving feelings she had denied herself for so long were swamping her common sense.

His kisses deepened, branding her with a promise of passion and male dominance. While one hand stroked her back with slow, sure movements, his other unbuttoned the halter and her bodice fell about her waist. His mouth leisurely traversed her neck, leaving a burning path in its wake, until he captured a hardened nipple between his teeth and nipped lovingly.

Rae was drowning in the exquisite sensuality of his caresses which touched her with deliberate slowness, as though they had all the time in the world to get to know every inch of each other.

When his mouth returned to cover hers, Rae was completely vulnerable to this man. Unknown sensations had taken over, and she felt more helpless now than ever before. She tried to grasp onto something to pull her up and out of the swirling whirlpool she found herself trapped in.

"Stay the night, Rae. You won't regret it," he moaned next to her parted lips. He seized them, the male insistence of his kiss pushing her closer and closer toward Jonathan. "I ache for you."

"Oh, Jonathan." Her voice was full of her own needs.

Lifting his head, he stared down at her, his cynically triumphant smile piercing the layers of desire he had woven around her and severing any bond she felt with him. Rae tore from the circle of his arms and hastily pulled her halter over her bare breasts. The glitter of male triumph vanished in his eyes. The rigid set of his shoulders and the uncompromising lines of his mouth and jaw revealed his growing anger. A deceptive calm cloaked her as her mantle of cool disdain, which had been cultivated over the years, fell into place.

Buttoning her dress Rae spoke with a haughty coldness. "The one thing I would regret most is staying the night. You've already designated yourself my business tutor. I don't think I want you to teach me anything else." Retrieving her purse and shawl Rae walked to the front door. "This relationship is only business, Mr. King. Please try to remember that in the future. During the time I'm forced to be associated with you, let's try to be civilized about this whole affair."

Then she hurriedly opened the door and escaped before he exploded. She was brave— to a point—and tonight she had pushed him too far. He would exact payment for that triumph. She had won this skirmish. The next time she might not be as lucky.

Fury mixed with frustration to race like searing fire through him, and Jonathan would gladly have throttled Rae; instead he balled his hands into tight fists until they ached from the strain. Then bringing one fist down upon a table, he shattered the stillness of the house.

"That woman will pay dearly," he muttered, and headed for the bar. He poured himself a double whiskey and downed it, but he still ached with an unfulfilled need. "Damn her!"

Turning to refill his glass he caught a glimpse of the fire burning in the fireplace and instantly the flames brought to mind a picture of Rae. She had taken him almost to the point of no return, then had left him standing there as though she had been the wronged one.

His anger still raged. He had been so close

to scaling her damned impregnable wall. So close!

If she thought he was a hard taskmaster these last few weeks, she hadn't seen anything yet. *Her lessons have only just begun, and by the time I get through with her she'll wish she'd never heard of me.*

Chapter Five

*R*ight now Rae would have liked nothing better than to tack the cover of *World Magazine* onto her wall and throw darts at Jonathan's arrogant face. She would have loved to bring him to his knees and make him regret ever throwing his weight around as if he owned the world.

This relationship wasn't working out! The last few weeks since the dinner party had been impossible. Savagely Rae tore the cover from the magazine, wadded his picture into a ball and tossed it into the wastebasket. *That's where he belongs—in the trash!*

Nothing she did pleased the opinionated perfectionist. It was as though he were determined to do the complete opposite of what she advised or wanted. He was deliberately making her life absolutely miserable.

For three weeks she had bitten back every retort that had sprung to her lips. She had been in her office at the crack of dawn and had stayed later than everyone else to try to be one step ahead of Jonathan. She knew what he was trying to do. He wanted to get her riled, but she wouldn't give him the pleasure of seeing her get angry. Instead, when she stepped through her apartment door, she vented her anger by calling him every name in the book to her poodle, Missi. After that ritual had finished, she was able to eat and finally relax before falling into bed.

Thank goodness for the first time in weeks Jonathan had gone back to Dallas for a while. A frown wrinkled her brows, though, as Rae ed his departure. He was so hard to figure out. Just as she was finally about to give him a piece of her mind, he had gone and done something unexpected. As he had left to catch his plane for Dallas, he had stuck his head into her office and told her to handle *everything*, not to bother him unless there was a crisis. Only a few hours before he had quietly called her down for not taking care of some details quickly enough on the new program they were developing. She had been so surprised by his new attitude that all she could do was stare at him as he left, a bright smile crinkling the corners of his eyes.

That had been five days ago and he was due back before ten this morning. Jonathan,

Shane, George and she were taking another group of investors to an oil field at ten-thirty.

Rising from her desk, Rae stretched her cramped muscles. This morning she had come into the office early again. The rigorous schedule she had been keeping since her father's death six weeks ago was beginning to show. She had lost over five pounds and the bright sparkle in her eyes was gone.

Exhausted, she made her way from her office to George's and nearly collapsed into the chair before his desk.

George scribbled something on a report, then leaned back in his chair, stroking his beard thoughtfully. "When are you going to slow down, Rae?"

"That's a good question. I suppose when I have learned everything."

"You'll be in the hospital before then. The company's doing all right. You're doing a fine job. Take a few days off and relax."

How could she tell him the company wasn't really in her hands? Jonathan never openly made the decisions. They always came through her, so everyone thought she managed Hamilton Oil, or at least managed it *jointly* with Jonathan.

She didn't know what kind of job she could do running it entirely on her own, since finance wasn't her field. The truth be known, she was pushing herself more than Jonathan. If she were able to prove to him she could manage Hamilton Oil, then maybe he would leave sooner than expected.

She didn't like what was happening to her

peaceful life since he had entered it. Nothing was the same, especially her feelings. Even when she was angry at him, excitement tingled through her if he touched her. And the worse part was that it was becoming strenuous to hide those feelings from him. It was taking all her years of experience to keep her distance and not to melt when he smiled at her in that certain way which warmed her to the tips of her toes.

"Rae?"

Rae looked up at George. "Sorry. I've had a lot on my mind lately."

"Take that vacation. That's the best advice a friend can give you. Tomorrow's Thursday. Take a long weekend. Go to the ranch. You love going there."

"No, not the ranch. It's still too soon after Dad's death."

"I'm sorry. I forgot that's where he was fishing. Well, then, go somewhere else or stay home."

"You know I can't. Those investors that Jonathan is bringing back from Dallas will probably have to be wined and dined tomorrow."

"He can handle it. He's a very capable man." George's eyes lit with mischief. "Isn't he?"

"He knows his business."

"Is that all?"

"I wouldn't know," Rae said in a crisp voice. "Now, did Susan check on those leases that were expiring?"

"Yes, and a few look promising. I'm checking into them, especially one near a well of ours. We've just been lucky that National Oil hasn't drilled on the land before now."

"You know how easily a land lease can get lost at a company and expire before the oil company has started drilling. I'm sure that's what happened."

"Yeah. That's happened to us a few times, too. It takes a lot of time to check out the land and stay on top of the leases that come up for renewal."

"That's one of the things I'm working on. I don't want Hamilton Oil accidentally losing a valuable lease again. I can still remember that piece of property we lost to Four Star Oil Company. How many barrels of oil does their well produce today?" Rae asked with a laugh.

"One hundred fifty barrels." Grimacing, George kneaded the back of his neck. "Don't remind me of that one. It sure could have helped the company a few years back. But then shortly after that your father got back on his feet."

By selling part of the company to Jonathan King, Rae thought bitterly. *A very costly mistake for me!*

A knock on the door ended their conversation. Jonathan stood in the doorway, his expression neutral.

A guarded smile was fixed on Rae's lips while involuntarily her gaze drank in his chiseled features. From across the room his masculinity seemed to blanket her with a suffocating intensity as his unwavering gaze made an impudent and slow tour of her body.

At the bold arrogance of his survey Rae turned back to George, her back stiff. *So the king is back to rule over his subjects*, she thought.

"Rae, I would like a word with you for a moment," Jonathan commanded, impatience heavy in his voice.

Surprise flashed in George's eyes as Rae's met them. Jonathan had never used that tone with her in front of the employees—only behind the closed door of her office. A pallor crept over her face. He was holding his temper for the benefit of George, but the effort was difficult and at any second it could be unleashed—*at her*.

"In your office. Now," Jonathan added curtly.

Slowly Rae stood on trembling legs. She knew why he was so angry. She had gone behind his back and halted the drilling on number two Jones and now she would pay dearly for getting caught. But she had hoped to convince him not to go past twelve thousand feet, and then it wouldn't have made any difference. She had tried to make him understand the risks involved these last few weeks, but he wouldn't budge from his decision. What had gotten into her head to go behind his back? She must be losing her mind, but *he was wrong to take the chance*.

As she walked past him she felt his eyes burn into the depths of her being with relentless fury. When the door to her office closed behind her, she stiffened in anticipation of his rage.

"What in the hell do you think you were doing telling the foreman on number two Jones to stop at that last sand? You knew I would find out. What in blazes were you trying to prove?" A rigid tension held him motionless, his mahogany-dark eyes scorching her where they insolently roamed.

The air seemed to snap with their strong emotions. A paralysis gripped her vocal cords and she couldn't speak, but they needed no words to communicate with one another.

Her eyes clashed with his. *Go to the devil,* hers telegraphed. *Not without you, my dear,* his replied.

They stood squarely facing each other for a full two minutes before Jonathan said tersely, "I want an answer, Rae. Before this, I at least credited you with some intelligence. I would have thought you were smart enough to know not to go against my wishes."

All the weeks of frustration and exhaustion that had pushed her control to the limit surfaced, and she could no longer remain silent. "Hamilton Oil is *my* company. I'll beg, borrow and even steal to get the money to buy your shares. Get the hell out of my life!" Her gray eyes turned bright and her chest rose and fell rapidly as she sucked in deep breaths.

Jonathan thrust his face into hers, his hands clenching her upper arms. "If you learn anything else, learn this, Rae. You can't change my mind once I've made it up. I don't back down. I resumed drilling on the well thirty minutes ago, and furthermore I made it perfectly clear who owns controlling interest in Hamilton Oil. That foolish foreman questioned my authority. He won't again." His grip tightened painfully. "Woman, you pushed me into making it clear to *my* staff who really runs this company. I had wanted to make it easier on you, but you made your bed. Now sleep in it."

Trying to ignore the bruising fingers digging into her flesh, Rae drew herself up to her full height, a coldness sweeping over her face like a sudden blizzard. "Then at least now I don't have to pretend anymore to the staff that I agree with your decision. They'll know where I stand, which is totally against you."

Jonathan hauled her against his iron strength, his mouth only an inch from hers, his hot breath tangling with hers. "Let me make it clear, lady. If you breathe one opposing word to anyone, you'll never own Hamilton Oil. I'll keep the damn shares to spite you."

"So your word doesn't really mean anything, after all."

He shoved her from him, insulting her with his contempt. "As far as I'm concerned your little scheme has severed any promises I made to you. Remember, you have to earn my respect, Rae, and you're doing a poor job of it."

Anger vibrated through her, making any coherent thought impossible. It took Rae several minutes to still the trembling that was threatening to take hold and to calmly say, "I don't have to earn anything because I don't

care what you think, Mr. King. Now, get out of
my office, if not out of my life."

Rae turned her back on him and waited
stiffly for him to leave, her breath suspended
in her lungs. A stress-filled moment passed
and Jonathan still stood behind her. She felt
his eyes drilling into her back and she suppressed the urge to leave her own office. *He
will not run me out of here,* she vowed silently.

"You think by ignoring me I'll go away."

Amusement now edged his voice and Rae
chanced a glance at him.

"Then you don't know me well at all, Rae.
Of course, we could change that. Have a late
dinner with me tonight." A roguish grin
spread across his features.

Rae swung around and glared at him. "Oh,
you're insufferable, Jonathan King. You'll try
anything to get your own way, won't you?
Well, you'll find you can't bully me, nor can
you sweet-talk me."

"In the weeks I've known you, Rae, I've
seen you let down that cool barrier of yours on
a number of occasions. You respond to me and
in your heart you know you can't deny it.
You're alive for the first time. You're fighting
it but you're no longer a machine programmed
only to work."

"Not only are you insufferable, but you're
egotistical, too. Is there no end to your many
talents?"

Jonathan threw back his head and laughed.
"And you, Rae Hamilton, are delightful. Will

you never learn to curb that sharp tongue of yours?"

"Probably not. I didn't know I had one until you came along. I rather like it," she retorted.

"I'll make a deal with you. I'll agree to a truce if you will."

She eyed him suspiciously. "Will you *really* listen to my opinions?"

"I'll listen."

"Okay."

Rae slowly extended her hand to shake on it. But Jonathan had other ideas. With a devilish glint in his eyes, he pulled her to him and kissed her, his tongue invading her mouth as he had invaded her life—forcibly and quickly. Before her mind could grasp onto a rational thought, her arms had stolen about him and she was returning his kiss. Shamelessly she molded her body to his, his hands massaging her until everything about them seemed liquid.

When their lips parted Rae felt abandoned. Jonathan pressed her head against his chest, and she listened to his quickened heartbeat. She affected him as he did her!

"Have dinner with me tonight, Rae. We can reach an acceptable agreement over Hamilton Oil. We don't have to be constantly at each other's throat."

His voice felt like velvet, caressing away any doubts or concerns she might have. She nodded her acceptance as she tried to master her reeling senses.

"Good. The sooner we show the investors

the oil field the sooner I can be alone with you." Jonathan planted a kiss on top of her head, then moved toward the door.

For a few seconds Rae wasn't sure if her legs would support her without his strength to lean into. But somehow she managed to accompany him to greet the three investors from Dallas. She was even able to answer all their questions sensibly on the two-hour drive to the oil field. However, this was extremely difficult because Jonathan sat next to her, giving her that warm smile every once in a while until she was sure the two men in the back heard her heart pounding against her breast.

When they reached the oil field, Rae greeted Shane, George and the third investor, then automatically started to talk business. But her mind dwelled on the evening to come. She was pointing out the various parts of the rig and explaining their function to one of the investors when she caught Jonathan staring at her with an utterly devastating look. She paused in midsentence, words drying in her throat.

"Miss Hamilton, is there anything wrong?" the investor asked.

"Huh? Oh, no. I'm sorry, Mr. Collins. Now, where was I?" She fought the urge to look again at Jonathan. With all her willpower she focused her full attention on the man near her and on her task.

But deep inside she felt her feelings changing, emotions shifting. She wasn't the woman of six weeks ago. She wasn't sure she liked the changes, but she was finding she had little control over what was happening to her. Jonathan had bulldozed his way into her life and now whether she wanted it or not he was an intricate part of it.

When the investor moved away to question the foreman, Rae stood still and tried to make some sense out of her turbulent thoughts. She became so engrossed that she didn't hear her name being shouted for a few seconds and the next thing she knew, Jonathan was hurling himself into her and slamming her to the ground. She started to jerk free, but a loud thud nearby froze her. Lying on the ground where she had been standing was a wrench that had fallen from the top of the ninety-foot derrick. Jonathan's eyes met hers, and silently she thanked him.

An eternity passed between them; in actuality only a moment. Then Jonathan was on his feet and helping her to stand on quivering legs. Her body shook as she stared at the metal wrench. She could have been seriously injured, or worse, killed. Jonathan had saved her life.

The trembling that was fast consuming her wouldn't stop. Jonathan gathered her to him and whispered soothing words. Everyone was watching them, but Rae didn't care. She pressed closer and drew strength from Jonathan. She had been at the rigs enough to know how dangerous they could be. A pipe could break loose from a cable or the man standing at the top of a derrick could drop something or accidentally knock something off, like a bolt or a wrench. If a person wanted a safe place to work, the oil rig wasn't it.

"Take several deep breaths, baby. You'll be all right." Jonathan tightened his arms about her, as though his embrace were a protective cocoon that shielded her from any danger.

When her heartbeat returned to its normal rate and the quaking subsided, Rae tilted her head back and smiled. "Thank you, Jonathan. I—"

He placed a finger over her lips. "You don't need to say anything else, Rae. I know. Let's get out of here. I think these men have seen all they want for one day. I want to get you home, baby."

On the long ride back to Tulsa, Rae felt numb, insulated in a vacuum. Jonathan's concern trapped her in a snare far more dangerous than she had ever thought possible. She could fight his superior male attitude; she had battled his type most of her life. But his gentleness was a completely different matter.

After seeing the men from Dallas off at the airport, Jonathan drove toward his house. When he parked his car in front of it, Rae finally spoke. "I thought the investors were staying until tomorrow."

"They informed me earlier that they had to be back in Dallas tonight, but would schedule another meeting next week."

"Oh, I see." An electrified silence grew between them.

Jonathan touched her cheek with a finger so

tenderly that it did more to undermine her than anything he had done in the past.

"Jonathan, I—"

"Come in, Rae."

The sensual look in his eyes tore down every stone she had placed around her heart. "Yes," she murmured before his mouth closed over hers, his hands framing her face.

"I won't be able to walk away, Rae. Do you understand, babe?"

Wordlessly she answered by kissing him with her own intense demands. She wanted it as much as he. She wanted to feel the comfort of his arms about her, to hear soft words of love whispered in her ear, to be wanted, desired and needed as a woman.

"Are we going to sit out in this car and negotiate all night, Jonathan?"

"No way, honey."

The walk up the steps to his front door seemed to take a lifetime. Now that Rae had committed herself there was no turning back. There was only an eagerness to feel and experience what had been building up in her for weeks.

Inside the door Jonathan immediately placed her purse and jacket on a table, then slipped his arms about her, urging her close to him with gentle insistence. The tasting exploration of his lips gave way to a stronger, more elemental pleasure as his mouth hungrily ravaged hers.

He swung her up into his arms and headed up the stairs and down a long hall. She had little time to inspect the masculine bedroom, done in different shades of brown with blue accents, before everything except the man near her was wiped from her mind. Placing her feet on the plush carpet, he smiled down at her with a male charm that played havoc with her already staggering senses.

Passion flared between them and flamed out of control while his lips traveled maddeningly slowly over her face, kissing her eyes, lips and nose before trailing down her neck to tease the tingling flesh at the base of her throat.

Moaning, Rae clung to him as he unbuttoned her blouse and unclasped her bra, then tantalized her nipples into throbbing points of desire. Lifting his head, he drew her to him with such fierceness that the air was driven from her lungs.

"You're so beautiful, Rae. I haven't been able to get you out of my mind since I first saw you. I believe you're a witch."

The soft, barely controlled steadiness of his voice sent her heart slamming against her rib cage, her pulse hammering through her veins. Jonathan made her feel every inch a woman, totally aware of herself, her beauty, her womanliness.

Jonathan slid her blouse down her arms, and it fell to the floor at her feet, followed immediately by her lacy bra. Standing back, he absorbed her beauty for a long, endless moment before he lightly ran his hand up from her waist, circling her breasts, and then returned to her waist.

Rae closed her eyes to savor the warm rapture in his touch, the heady male scent that was like an erotic stimulant arousing her to a mindless ecstasy. Slipping his fingers between her and the waistband, he moved around to unfasten the skirt in the back, the linen material quickly joining her other clothes on the floor.

She in turn boldly worked the buttons on his silk shirt loose and proceeded to undress him at a delightfully torturous pace. For a short time she felt in control with this man whose breathing was becoming ragged, whose very presence threw her otherwise sensible mind into chaos.

He stilled her teasing caresses, which fleetingly grazed his hard male contours, and took her mouth in a savage possession which claimed as its rights what no other man had been granted. He tunneled his fingers through her hair, tangling them in the flaming strands as he rained kisses over her face, never seeming to get enough.

"Rae." A wealth of emotions was communicated in that one word as he swept her up into his arms and carried her the few remaining feet to the bed, where he settled her on the velour softness of his coverlet.

Towering over her, Jonathan paid homage to her loveliness while Rae studied him in return. His face was compelling, lean and strong. His thighs were muscled columns of male power and his body in motion had a masculine elegance which left the vivid impression of a primitive, lethal strength just under the civilized veneer.

His thumb continued its absorbing survey, touching her mouth and slowly outlining it with a disturbing sensuality. He was attacking her with sensuous ease, and she thrilled beneath his mind-shattering caresses. Her passion-filled eyes locked with his and were mesmerized by the probing force of his dark gaze, which seemed to be searching for her true, buried feelings. But from the minute he had touched her in the car, she had laid bare her heart and soul to him. Her vulnerability reached out and beckoned to him.

Jonathan knelt on the bed beside her, then fitted his length along hers. *My God, she is beautiful,* he thought. Not even in his wildest dreams had he thought she would respond so ardently. She was like fire and ice, and he knew in that moment he wouldn't be able to walk away from her until he knew her thoroughly, body and soul. She stirred some inner emotion in him that only increased his fascination. It would be difficult to forget her.

His mouth found hers with seductive sureness. Leisurely Jonathan kissed a singeing path down her neck to her breasts, exciting them to hardness with his tongue.

"Oh, please, Jonathan," Rae moaned softly, a swirling, velvet mist of sensations enveloping her. "Now!" The exquisite ache deep inside sent her nerve ends screaming with a great need for his possession.

He moved up until he captured her lips, nibbling the lower one. His searching fingers continued to adore her while the hungry plunder of his mouth elicited a fevered reaction.

"No, babe. There's still much to learn," he murmured while nuzzling erotically at the hypersensitive skin of her neck.

The tenderness in his kiss didn't prepare her for his next movement. One hand roamed down her body, deliberately, slowly and stopped finally to stroke her through her panties, then moved beneath the silky material, removing her last garment.

Rae arched toward him, wanting him to end this sweet torture, the unfamiliar sensations too much for her. Wherever his hand traveled, it left a fiery trail. Whenever his mouth claimed hers, she became even more attuned to him, a marvelously delicious feeling.

She wanted to explore every inch of him. The teasing suggestion of her fingers insolently roved over his muscled body, tormenting him until he could do nothing but end this madness.

The tempest of their completion was wildly frenzied, as if their lives had been destined for this one night. Finally sated, Jonathan reached out for Rae and folded her tightly, tenderly to him. With the back of his hand he stroked her cheek gently, making it hard to bring her breathing back to normal.

Everything was changed, and yet nothing was different. They were still on opposing sides where Hamilton Oil was concerned. She didn't know where anything stood anymore. For someone who had mapped out her whole life, it was an unnerving sensation.

"Stay the night, Rae. This is much more enjoyable than fighting. I can take care of you."

Wandering in a maze of emotional confusion, Rae listened to the possessive ring that entered his voice. Take care of her? Why couldn't people leave her alone and not try to run her life? Why did she feel she had to mold her life to fit someone else's expectations? First her father and now Jonathan. He didn't share; Jonathan dominated. *And I will not be dominated!*

Rae sat up and looked down at Jonathan. "I have to go."

"Why?" There was an implacable steel edge to that one word.

"I have my own place, Jonathan."

"And I'm sure you've spent the night away from it." He rose now and stared down at her.

"That's not it."

"I know, Rae. Give me credit for knowing some things about you. You're scared. I've awakened feelings in you that you didn't realize existed."

Angry at his male pride and the truth behind his words, Rae scrambled from his bed and faced him with her cool mask in place. "Don't flatter yourself. I won't deny I enjoyed our little—romp, but now it's time to leave. Will you drive me or must I call a cab?"

A murderous look pierced her. His eyes took on the aspect of cold marble, his features carved granite.

"I'll drive you. That's the least I can do after

that delightful—*romp*. Now, go get dressed, my dear."

Rae hurriedly gathered her clothes and fled into his bathroom, quickly dressing before she changed her mind. The scorn in his expression cut deep into her and hurt. Why couldn't someone take the time to look beneath the facade she presented to the world? Why couldn't she drop that "I can do it alone" front for someone to get close? It was a habit she couldn't shed overnight and wasn't sure she even wanted to.

When she reentered his bedroom, he lay stretched out on his bed, fully dressed, his hands casually crossed behind his head. Nothing seemed to get to him for long. She had thwarted his plans for the night, but that was all. This evening would fade quickly from his memory, while instinctively Rae sensed she would remember his lovemaking for years to come.

"Let's go," he said as he swung his legs to the floor and stood.

The short, silent ride to her apartment gnawed further at Rae's already frazzled nerves. The second he brought his car to a stop, she opened the door and ran up the stairs.

Jonathan waited until she was inside, a frustrated tension in every fiber of his being. He had said the wrong thing to her. He had seen the trapped look in her eyes. He slammed his hand into the steering wheel. But damn it, he wasn't moving too fast. He had held a tight rein on his desire for weeks—*long, agonizing weeks*. As he jerked the car into drive, he vowed to erase the little witch from his mind. He would exorcise her from him and end this roller-coaster ride he found himself on. It would be strictly business between them from now on.

Chapter Six

*R*ae stared out her window at the parking lot below, mentally trying to prepare herself for another confrontation with Jonathan over a deep well that had recently run into some serious problems. These last six weeks since the night they had made love, the atmosphere between them had definitely been chilly.

As she reflected back over the success of number two Jones, she was astonished to realize she had wanted it to fail. Hamilton Oil would have lost thousands of dollars, but to have been able to tell Jonathan "I told you so" would have been worth it.

That certainly isn't a very professional attitude, Rae Hamilton, she told herself, but her feelings toward Jonathan were absolutely confusing, making her life very complicated.

Of course, it didn't really make any difference, since his attraction toward her had unquestionably abated. Yet, trying to convince herself that she was now relieved only depressed her.

Memories of the night they had made love constantly inundated her thoughts. Those memories were like a narcotic; she kept going back for more in larger doses.

She had found herself daydreaming at the oddest times—in a staff meeting, on the phone to the field or in the middle of a conversation with a department head. One thing was for sure—Jonathan King wasn't helping her concentration!

Well, she would just have to make a more determined effort to banish him from her thoughts. The sooner he returned to Dallas *for good*, the sooner she could get on with her life and run Hamilton Oil the way *she* wanted to. It would feel great to be entirely her own person again.

Shrugging off the depression that was taking hold, Rae turned from the window, her gaze drawn toward the connecting door between their offices. Why did she feel that door was more than a passageway? It was as if it linked her to him in a very concrete, permanent way.

The phone ringing jolted her away from her disquieting thoughts, and she reached to answer it.

"Rae, I'll pick you up at your apartment at eight," Shane said.

"Make it eight-thirty and I'll be there ready to paint the town red." She forced a light tone into her voice, but her eyes remained a dark gray.

"Working late *again*."

"You aren't going to lecture me *again*." This time a genuine smile curved her lips.

"No. I'm saving my breath. Until eight-thirty."

After placing the receiver back on its cradle, Rae glanced at her watch. Six-thirty. Jonathan should be through with his meeting by now. She made her way toward the connecting door, a firm resolve in her long, purposeful strides.

Knocking once, she entered as Jonathan looked up from reading a report. Somehow she had to make him see her side of this issue. He was gambling with *her* company, *her* future.

There was a wariness in the atmosphere and in his eyes. "Yes? I thought you had already gone home."

"I rarely leave my office before seven-thirty. Today is no different." Her voice was cool. She sat down in a chair in front of his desk and leaned back, determined to appear calm, while inside her nerves were frazzled. She felt as though she had been walking a tightrope these last three months and it was beginning to wear her down.

Amusement lit his dark eyes. "Well, is all this hard work and devotion worth it? Do you think you'll be able to get rid of me sooner?"

"Aren't you better equipped to answer that question than I am? After all, what I want counts little in this *partnership*."

"Now, there you're wrong. I listen to everything you say—"

"Then do what you please."

"Not always, Rae. We just don't see eye to eye on some of the bigger issues. You're too conservative."

"And you're going to change all that," she retorted without thinking. Jonathan's eyes glinted with a suppressed smile and Rae quickly continued in a frosty voice, "There's nothing wrong with being conservative, especially when so much money is involved."

"But there's such a thing as taking a calculated risk with the odds in your favor. When you understand the financial aspects of this business better, I think you'll see my side of things."

"And when you understand the engineering aspects better, you'll see *my* side of the situation," she countered, anger beginning to heat her voice.

A mocking lift of one eyebrow restrained her hot temper, and again an aloof composure returned to her voice.

"This is why I need to see you. To explain my views on number one McIntosh."

"I wondered when you would get around to seeing me about that well." Amusement still lurked in the midnight depths of Jonathan's eyes.

"A sidetrack is too costly. Mechanically I

think it's extremely risky. I recommend we plug the hole and abandon it now."

For a second a pleading tone had entered Rae's voice, but she quenched it quickly. She wouldn't beg. When facing the opponent, she had to present her case dispassionately and calmly, as her father had taught her. Never before had she had such a hard time keeping her poise, but then never before had she met anyone like Jonathan King.

"If there's gas below the fifteen-thousand-foot level we're at now, as we strongly suspect, we'll make a lot of money on the deregulated gas. The gas potential more than offsets the risk of the sidetrack failing. That is, *if* it fails, and there's a good chance it won't. I think the situation warrants the risk, Rae."

"And if I say it doesn't?" Tension made her temples throb as she straightened in her chair. "The probability of a successful sidetrack is slim at that depth. Let's go ahead and redrill a new hole next to the old one. It's less risky."

"You could be right, but with the profits from number two Jones we can afford to take the chance. I would rather gamble that the sidetrack will work and only spend half a million, than squander millions to redrill in that field."

"You'll have to in the end anyway, and we'll be out the half a million on top of the redrilling costs." His cool logic threatened to snap her tenuous control. Again he was ignoring her opinion and doing what he wanted.

"I gave the go-ahead this afternoon, Rae."

Rising, she said in a crisp voice, "I see I've wasted my time *again*."

Rae was halfway across his office when his next sentence halted her. "Will you have dinner with me tonight? You shouldn't work late every night, Rae."

"I don't notice you going home early. Besides, I have a goal in mind. Remember?"

"Ah, yes." A smile crinkled the corners of his eyes. "Getting rid of me. You wound my male ego, Rae Hamilton."

"That is the chance a person must take when he waltzes into someone's life and messes it up completely. I thought you liked to take risks, anyway."

"Correction. Only a calculated risk when the odds are in *my* favor."

The devastating look on his face clearly underscored the real meaning behind his words. She presented a challenge to him, but one he definitely thought he could conquer.

"You haven't answered me, Rae."

With immense pleasure, she said, "Sorry. I already have a dinner date with Shane."

"Is it business or pleasure?" he taunted.

"Since it's none of your business, I'll let you wonder. But for your information I am interested in more than Hamilton Oil." She tossed the last sentence over her shoulder as she left his office, his low chuckle greeting her ears through the closed door.

Inside her own office, Rae stared at the stack of unread papers on her desk. "Why bother," she muttered to herself, and retrieved her purse from the bottom drawer of her desk before heading down the hall.

As she was stepping onto the elevator, she heard Jonathan call out, "Wait up, Rae."

For a brief second she hesitated, then punched the "Door Open" button.

"I see you've decided to call it an early evening after all," Jonathan said as the doors swished shut behind him, confining them together in the small elevator.

"Seven isn't exactly early."

With Jonathan so close to her, clearly content with his present situation, Rae was very relieved when the doors finally opened onto the ground floor. Quickly she crossed the lobby and stepped out into the warm spring air. Jonathan's musky male scent lingered in her nostrils, making it hard for her to dismiss his dark gaze from her thoughts.

A firm hand on her arm swung her around. She tried to pull free, but Jonathan held her securely.

"This is after hours and I don't intend to be bullied by you anymore today, Mr. King."

"*Rae*, I wanted to tell you that I agree with your evaluation on number three David. You're right and I see no use in drilling any further."

He released her, but she didn't move away, confused that he had gone out of his way to tell her the news. She knew he could have sent her a memo or let her find out from Shane. But he hadn't. Was he trying to pacify her because of the deep well, or was he genuinely trying to tell her he was listening to her opinions? It was impossible to divine his real motive. It would be easier on her if she believed he valued her opinion, but she had always been taught to trust very few people.

"Don't look so shocked, Rae." A wicked playfulness touched his eyes. "I haven't completely amended my high-handed ways. Since you're seeing Shane tonight, I thought it best that you know about the well. He might mention it and I wouldn't want you to appear too stunned."

"Why the consideration *now?*" Mock surprise flitted across her features.

He shortened the distance between them in two strides. "I have always considered your feelings, Rae. I'm not the blackguard you think I am."

It was her turn to arch a brow. "Aren't you? Is that why everyone knows you're the *senior* partner in this partnership? You've made it quite plain in the last six weeks."

A suggestion of tautness in his body indicated he wasn't entirely unaffected by her accusation. Quickly, though, all traces of strain were erased from his expression as he answered, "If you hadn't openly challenged me on number two Jones that wouldn't have been necessary. I was perfectly willing to be a *silent senior* partner. You're the one who set that rule down and now you must live with it."

"Did you really think I could stand by and watch you do something I thought was wrong for the company, *my company?*"

"That's where you're wrong. You keep

thinking of Hamilton Oil as your company. It's *our* company, Rae, and the sooner you face that fact the easier things will be between us."

"All I represent to you is a challenge, Jonathan King, and you're the type of man who can't walk away until you have dominated and conquered. Why don't you save your valuable time and let me have my company back?"

His virility was encompassing her, his fire raging inside of her. Only a few inches were between them, causing sensuous impressions to ravish her thoughts. A throbbing desire for him again blazed to life as she relived their ardent lovemaking in her mind. The sensations he had created in her six weeks ago hadn't diminished with time.

"Damnit! Quit saying *my* company!" Jonathan said in a terse voice.

With one swift movement he anchored her to him, riveting her senses on the tactile warmth of his body, the gentle roughness of his touch and his pleasing male scent.

"I want you, Rae Hamilton, and I will have you. That night we made love *will not* be a one-night stand."

His hand came up to brush a wayward strand of hair from her face, its soft, light touch on her cheek managing at the same time to communicate the potential power of his grip.

What would it be like if Jonathan King lost complete command of himself, Rae wondered as his mouth opened over hers, his tongue urging her lips to allow him free access to the sweet recesses of her mouth. For a moment she couldn't muster any resistance to his tender persuasion as he weaved a web of ownership over her. It enveloped her, absorbed her until she felt herself drowning in his dominance.

Catching him off guard, she pulled away. "I may not have a choice in the matter of business, but my personal life remains my own. And you definitely have no say in it!"

Her breasts were heaving as she drew air into her lungs to still the rapid beating of her heart.

"You're right, Rae. I don't walk away from a challenge."

"Don't you understand you're making it impossible for us to work together." She fought to keep a desperate tone from her voice. She felt her life wasn't her own anymore and she didn't know what to do about it.

"Why? I think we make a good team. I can separate my business from my personal life. As far as I'm concerned, what we develop personally between us will not affect our working partnership. Are you having trouble separating the two?"

"Stay away from me." Exasperation mingled with anger.

"Is that a plea from someone who knows she has lost the war?"

"I have lost nothing except my company." She regarded him with a grim hardness that sharpened her eyes to two pinpoints.

Laughter pealed from his chest. "Oh, Rae,

you're exceptionally beautiful when you're angry. And you're very stubborn." He reached out and ran his hand lightly down her arm. "I'll see you tomorrow morning. Have a nice evening."

Rae watched as he strode toward his Mercedes, rage immobilizing her. She shook off the paralyzing feeling and started for her own car. The air about her still crackled with their intense emotions, and she still felt his nearness deep within.

He is so sure of himself! No one can dominate me. No one!

Even with her father Rae had always maintained her independence. Besides, her father had always listened to her and valued her opinion.

On the drive to her apartment, the scene between Jonathan and her played over and over in her mind like a broken record. Her thoughts kept returning to his kiss and a tingling warmth began to curl through her. Her grip on the steering wheel tightened until pain shot up her arms. Determinedly, she made herself relax as she parked her car, let herself into her apartment and fixed herself a glass of white wine. Sipping her drink, she began to dress for her date with Shane, taking extra care to look nice.

If it were the last thing she did, she would forget Jonathan King. He was not going to ruin this evening. She so rarely went out anymore; there never seemed to be any time with all the work she had to do.

By the time she was ready all emotional

effects of the confrontation with Jonathan were wiped from her expression. In a beige silk dress she felt confident she didn't look one bit like an executive, a bolstering thought.

Precisely at eight-thirty Shane rang the doorbell. He prided himself on his punctuality, Rae remembered as she opened the door.

"Now, I like that dress, boss." A low whistle was emitted from Shane's lips.

"Well, thank you. I needed that." Rae stepped aside to allow Shane to walk into the apartment. "Do you want a drink before we go?"

"That sounds great. A whiskey and soda, please."

Moving toward the bar Rae asked, "Rough day?"

"Lately that's all there has been. Jonathan King is tough to work for. He demands a lot from his employees."

Rae paused in the middle of pouring the whiskey, her mouth compressed into a thin line. *Even Shane feels it's Jonathan's company now. Can't I be rid of that man for at least one night?*

"You know, we've never talked about him taking over, Rae. We've been so busy lately I haven't had much chance to talk with you, period. Is everything okay?"

Rae finished making Shane his drink, then fixed herself one, all the time composing her thoughts. "This is only a temporary arrangement, so I'll survive." *I think,* she added silently.

"I see he decided to drill a sidetrack on

number one McIntosh. That will cost a great deal and might not do the trick."

Rae set her glass down hard, her expression stern. "May we talk about something else besides Jonathan King? I want to enjoy myself this evening."

"Sure, Rae, but if you need someone to talk to, I'm always available."

"Thanks, but I can handle Mr. King."

Later that night as Rae was preparing for bed, she remembered her brave words to Shane. *I can handle Mr. King.* She laughed at the impossible situation she found herself in. Right now she was beginning to feel she couldn't handle anything—Hamilton Oil, her traitorous body or one Jonathan King.

Chapter Seven

"What's this on my desk?" Rae stopped half-way across her office, staring at her desk in puzzlement.

"Looks like a rose to me," Shane teased. "One perfect, long-stemmed white rose."

"I didn't know you took horticulture in college."

Suddenly Rae wished Shane hadn't accompanied her to her office for that report on number one McIntosh. Some sixth sense told her who had sent the exquisite-looking rose in a silver bud vase. *Jonathan!*

Rae started for her desk again and picked up the folder with the McIntosh report in it. "Here. I'll see you at the staff meeting this afternoon." Her tone dismissed Shane and discouraged any further discussion of the rose.

When the door closed behind Shane, Rae turned slowly toward her desk and touched the perfect white bud. A faint, sweet fragrance permeated the air.

Why? What's he up to now?

Rae fingered the small white envelope propped up next to the vase, then quickly opened it to confirm what she already knew in her heart.

Please, have lunch with me?

Jonathan

His bold signature leaped off the paper and filled her with a sense of foreboding.

"Well, will you, Rae?"

Spinning around, she sucked in a deep breath at the sight of Jonathan lounging against the door frame between their offices. An ensuing tension filtered rapidly through the room like billowing smoke. Even though on the surface he appeared nonchalant, thoroughly relaxed, there was an aura of wiry toughness about him which alerted Rae that his restrained power was leashed now, but promised to be released later.

Her wariness grew.

"It's not often I find you at a loss for words." Humor brightened his dark eyes.

Rae sensed a subtle change in him as Jonathan pushed himself away from the doorjamb and in one fluid motion shut the door and started toward her. She held her ground even though warning signals were flashing in her mind.

Finally she replied in a detached voice, "Which is this luncheon date? Business mixed with pleasure? Or pleasure mixed with business?"

"Neither. It's strictly *pleasure*." Jonathan glanced at his watch. "And you have ten minutes to give me your answer."

"Ten minutes?"

"It's ten till eight. At eight your time belongs to Hamilton Oil."

His voice was rough and warm at the same time, and Rae was disoriented for a few seconds as she digested this new aspect to the situation between them. He had paused a few feet from her and was keeping his distance on purpose. There was none of the tough arrogance in his voice that she had detected last night. Instead she sensed a change of tactics, a softening that was just as dangerous to her peace of mind.

Confusion furrowed her brow. "I don't think—"

"Rae, I've been wrong these past few months. I entered your life at a difficult time. I tried to bulldoze you into submitting, into having an affair with me."

A troubled look replaced his relaxed regard. This apology wasn't coming easy to Jonathan, Rae thought, and felt a sense of power in recognizing it.

"I'm sorry for handling this situation all

wrong. My only excuse is that you're different from most women. I'm used to protecting, dominating—and even at times bullying."

"And you've finally realized those techniques don't work on me."

"Sometimes I amaze myself. Usually I'm not this slow to learn."

The distance between them diminished, but he didn't try to touch her. A gentle smile crept over his features as he stared down into her gray eyes.

"You're special, Rae. I want to start over with you." He extended his right hand toward hers. "I'm Jonathan King."

She looked at his proffered hand, then back at his face, laughter suddenly bubbling from her throat. "I'm Rae Hamilton." Her hand was enclosed in his large one, the feel of his touch no less disturbing than his mere presence.

"It's a *pleasure* to meet you, Rae Hamilton. Will you please have lunch with me?" His expression was the picture of innocence, but his eyes danced with mischief.

His smile was infectious and it took a great deal of willpower not to melt into his arms, to surrender to the blissful sensations she knew he could produce.

But a change of tactics doesn't really make any difference, Rae firmly told herself. A relationship with him would be a deadend.

Slowly she shook her head and stepped back until she felt the desk press into her legs. "It still wouldn't work, Jonathan. I've lived and breathed this business for years. How can I separate the two now when I'm fighting *with you* to retain control?"

Again only inches were between them, his vibrant masculinity like an electrical current flowing from him and passing through her.

"Come to lunch with me and I'll show you. Hamilton Oil won't be mentioned once the whole time. I want to get to know Rae Hamilton the woman, not the drilling engineer."

Her throat closed as she looked into his eyes, mesmerizing, steadfast. Deep in his eyes she saw the silent challenge he dared her to accept. Was she willing to get to know Jonathan King the man?

Softly his voice penetrated her thoughts. "Two minutes till eight, Rae."

This was all so ridiculous! What did she have to lose? Surely she could keep her emotional distance. It could only help her situation with Hamilton Oil if they became friends. She might even learn how to get around this man and make him see her side of things.

"Okay. I'll go." Her answer was emitted in a breathless whisper.

"Good. We'll leave at eleven-thirty unless you have an appointment that will interfere."

"No. I'm free then."

Pulling away a few feet, Jonathan became serious, a businesslike expression on his face now. "Well, it's time we get to work, Miss Hamilton. I need to see those reports on the Jones field in Woodward County."

Rae straightened and moved behind her desk, her professional, aloof mask falling into place. "I'll have them for you in an hour, Mr. King."

He strode to the connecting door, but paused before opening it and glanced over his shoulder at her, devilment in his eyes. "Make that forty-five minutes, Miss Hamilton."

"Yes, sir," Rae muttered as the door closed.

The atmosphere was still charged with his essence, his heady male scent saturating the air and mingling with the fragrance of the white rose. No man had ever sent her flowers —correction, flower—and she couldn't help the pleased expression that softened her features. It made her feel special, every inch a woman. She had fought so hard to play down her femininity in the field that now it felt wonderful to be reminded of it.

The intercom buzzed. "Yes, Mrs. Daniels." Rae set the bud vase to the side and opened a folder. "I'll see him now."

From that moment on she had no time to daydream or contemplate what Jonathan was up to. As usual she had so much work to do that she didn't realize where the time had gone when Jonathan knocked, then entered her office, at eleven-thirty.

"Right on time. You're a man after my own heart."

A crooked grin slid across his mouth. "I have no intention of wasting one minute of this hour, Rae. You've made it quite clear there's to be a strict division of business and pleasure hours."

"That's the only way this situation can work."

"It's never been a problem before."

"I can take that two ways. Either you've never wanted to date a female associate or there haven't been any female colleagues. Which is it?" Retrieving her purse, Rae rose, her gaze trained on Jonathan, watching his expression intently.

"I think that's a loaded question, Rae Hamilton."

"Well, it's only fair. If you're going to get to know me better, then I should get to know you, too."

Laughter filled the office. "Somehow I don't think your reasons for getting to know me are the same as mine. Are you looking for ammunition to use against me?" Jonathan stood aside and opened the door for her.

Passing near him Rae felt that electrical current recharge and leap between them. She hurried through her outer office and didn't stop until she was in front of the elevator, where Jonathan paused a foot too close for her peace of mind.

"Are you an equal opportunity employer?" Rae asked, and stepped onto the elevator, standing as far from him as the four walls would permit.

But even at a distance he invaded her mind, her thoughts a riot of conflicting feelings. Part of her didn't care what he said as long as she could listen to his husky baritone voice; her other half cautioned her, reciting a list of characteristics she wanted in a man.

"Yes, but none of my right-hand people are females."

"I'm not surprised," Rae replied as she walked out of the elevator and headed toward the glass doors.

Outside, Jonathan's hand closed around her upper arm, stopping her progress toward his car. "Are you accusing me of being a chauvinistic employer?"

"Well, are you?" She met his direct look with her own daring one.

"I will not apologize to you for the fact that I have three assistants, all men, with whom I work directly. They have been with me for years, and in fact two of them had been with my father for years. I have female executives at King Industries and have never hesitated to hire the opposite sex when she is qualified." He propelled her toward his Mercedes, the door slamming closed slightly harder than necessary after Rae slid into the car.

His strides were rigid as he rounded the front of the car, his expression set in grim lines as he climbed in, none of the tenseness leaving his face.

"Why won't you let me run Hamilton Oil? Is it because I'm a woman?"

Rae's question sliced through the thick air and brought Jonathan around to stare at her with a dangerous calm.

"I thought this luncheon date was for pleasure. I don't call getting the third degree about my hiring practices pleasurable. Why do *you* insist on discussing business?"

"Because that question has been bothering me and I want to know the truth. If there's to be any kind of—friendship between us, and at this point that is doubtful—I must know where I stand."

His eyes drilled into her with a steadfast purpose that was suffocating. "There was a time in the beginning when I briefly contemplated letting Raymond's heir run the company if I thought *he* was capable. I was under the impression that you were male." His gaze raked the length of her, missing nothing.

And how wrong I was, his eyes told her.

"Probably because my father wanted a son so badly that sometimes he forgot I was a daughter." Sadness invaded her voice, but she quickly concealed it.

Jonathan's eyes narrowed and searched her now masked features. "Whatever the reason, I was surprised to find out you were a female. My initial response was to buy the shares because you were a female, but later, after reading a report on you, I realized your education by your father was incomplete. I decided I would finish it for him while I protected my investment. Besides, by then I was intrigued, Rae. You had definitely caught my interest. I haven't had that happen to me in a long time."

Rae ignored the suggestiveness of his last sentence, making herself concentrate only on the fact that he had invaded her privacy. "You had a report done on me?"

"Of course. Would you have done any differently if you were me?"

She felt violated, as if nothing were private anymore. He was slowly picking her life apart.

"Yes! No, it was a good business move, but that fact doesn't make it any pleasanter for me to swallow."

Jonathan started the engine and maneuvered the Mercedes from the parking lot. "I hadn't meant to reveal that, but you wanted the truth. And I want only the truth between us."

Rae glanced at him. "You know you do have a trace of the chauvinistic attitude in you."

"Yes, I know, but I'll try to keep it under wraps." He threw her a smile that teased her and sent her pulse racing. "I thought we'd eat at the Williams Center since we're pressed for time."

"May I choose the restaurant?"

"If you like."

They lapsed into a comfortable silence while Jonathan negotiated the heavy lunchhour traffic in downtown Tulsa. After parking next to the Williams Center, Jonathan placed his arm casually around Rae's waist and began walking toward the complex of restaurants and stores. A strong urge to move from his loose embrace assailed her, but she didn't. His hold was light but binding.

"Which restaurant, Rae? I wouldn't want to be accused of being domineering." Jonathan paused inside the doors, a smile creasing the corners of his eyes.

"I'm in the mood for pizza. Let's eat by the skating rink."

"Among the *hundreds* of other people trying to eat at noontime."

His amused tone clearly divulged that he

had read through her strategy. She didn't want to be alone with him in a quaint restaurant that would afford them some privacy, even at this hectic time of day.

After moving through the cafeteria line, Jonathan directed Rae to a table for two overlooking the ice rink. It was near a large wooden planter set off slightly from the others around them, and was as private as possible under the circumstances. *Leave it to Jonathan to find the best table in the place*, Rae thought as she sat down.

"Do you skate?" *That ought to be a safe enough topic.*

"No." Jonathan's mouth quirked into a half smile. "Do you?"

"No."

They both burst out laughing, bringing stares from the people at the nearby tables.

"If I let you have your way, Rae, we would exchange polite greetings in the morning and that would be all."

"Polite?"

"Is wary a better word?"

"Maybe."

A warmth covered her as his devilish regard traveled over her. Quickly she began to eat; she had to do something with her trembling hands.

Looking out onto the ice rink, Rae watched a man in a business suit as he skated in circles. Then, tiring of watching the businessman, she swung her gaze upward, silently counting the exposed levels fronting the atrium, all overlooking the rink. She felt Jonathan's eyes on her and was reluctant to pull her gaze from the milling shoppers.

"Rae, I have a favor to ask of you."

Her attention swerved back to Jonathan. "A favor?" she asked guardedly.

"Yes. Will you help me pick out a birthday gift for my mother? Her birthday is Friday and I haven't the slightest idea what to get her."

"I gather she has everything."

"And then some."

She didn't want to become any more engrained in Jonathan's life than she already was, but there was a genuinely helpless look on his face that reached out to her.

"I used to have a hard time shopping for my father's birthday. I'll help as much as I can, but I don't think I can be of much assistance. I don't know her tastes."

"Expensive and elegant. She's delicate and dainty. The typical arts patron and social matron."

Like my mother had been, Rae thought, then said aloud, "Well, we can give it a shot after we eat."

There had been a part of her that had wanted to be like her mother, totally feminine, while the other part had battled to please her father, which had meant quenching some of those traits. There had been no time for tears, talk of dates and what to wear to parties with girlfriends and, most of all, no dependence on anyone. Emotions hadn't been allowed to rule her life and for the most part had had to be suppressed. Rae dismissed thoughts of the past and the war she had fought within herself. What good did it do to dwell on it?

They hurriedly finished their pizzas, then took the escalator up to the top level where some of the stores were. As they browsed in several shops, suggestion after suggestion was discarded for one reason or another by Jonathan.

Pausing in front of an expensive gift shop, Rae braced her hands on her hips and asked in an exasperated tone, "Are you sure you wanted my help?"

"Yes. Just because I can tell you what she wouldn't like doesn't necessarily mean I can tell you what she would like."

"Okay, but this has to be the last place. We're already on company time."

Merriment sparkled in his eyes. "I think we can extend our lunch hour this one time. We've certainly earned it these last few months." He leaned close to her and added, "I won't tell the boss if you won't."

"I don't know. I feel a certain loyalty to him."

Jonathan started to laugh. "I just bet you do. Come on. Let's see what this shop has to offer."

Inside the store Rae's attention was immediately drawn to a delicate porcelain ballerina sitting in a glass case. It was perfect. Her mother would have loved it.

"I've got just the gift for your mother, Jonathan," Rae said as she pulled him across the room to stand in front of the case. She pointed triumphantly toward the ballerina figure, poised in an arabesque.

Jonathan's critical gaze appraised it; then in a delighted voice he announced, "You've done it again, babe."

The endearment took her by surprise, and her heartbeat increased. The atmosphere suddenly became intimate, his eyes locking with hers in a wordless message of thanks.

Blinking, Rae broke the spell. "We have a staff meeting this afternoon, so I suggest you buy the figurine and we get back to the office. It wouldn't do for the bosses to be late."

"Oh, never that!" Mockery tinged his voice, but he quickly commandeered a saleslady and bought the porcelain ballerina.

Nothing else was said until they were settled in his Mercedes and on their way back to the office. His eventual question took Rae entirely by surprise. "Will you fly down to Dallas with me Thursday night? We're having a small celebration Friday for Mother."

"That's not possible," Rae answered in a whisper, shock registering in her voice.

"Why?"

She sensed his sudden stiffening and knew he was instinctively preparing for a battle. "Because, Jonathan, I have work to do."

"And it will still be there on Monday."

There was a tightening of the electrical charge between them and Rae marshaled her defenses. "No. I can't." She interjected a firmness into her denial.

"I don't have to be hit with a sledgehammer. I get the picture." Jonathan drove the car into his reserved parking space, turned the engine off, then focused his full attention on Rae. Her pulse increased its tempo. The seductive darkness of his eyes played havoc with her senses as the unmistakable desire in him became a commanding force that touched her soul.

Her mounting passion couldn't be denied as his fingertips massaged the back of her neck with enticing delicacy. Heat flickered in her loins, and she felt as if her muscles were turning to liquid.

Finally she found her voice. "We're on Hamilton Oil's time now. Remember, strictly business."

Jonathan's hand dropped away but his dark gaze fastened onto hers with a male appeal. "If you won't go with me to Dallas, then at least rescue me from a dull lawn party on Sunday."

She shook her head, afraid her voice would only be a weak thread.

"You can't let me go to this party without a date. I have an image to uphold in front of my kid sister. Her boyfriend is giving it." Jonathan's grin was positively rakish, tempering her reluctance.

"Oh, poor man and you don't know any other women in town."

"None—that is, as beautiful, tempting and alluring as you." He took her hand, his fingers toying with hers. "I won't let you leave until you agree. You can't completely destroy my male ego and refuse two dates with me. I may never recover."

She needed desperately to escape the small confines of his car before she did agree to accompany him to both functions. Deciding to accept the lesser of two temptations, Rae said, "I'll go with you to the lawn party then. I certainly wouldn't want the staff to see us conducting a—conference in your car without them."

"Oh, positively improper, Miss Hamilton," Jonathan said as he got out of the car and started walking toward the office building. Inside the lobby he added, "I have to talk to George, so I'll see you at the staff meeting later."

He began walking away, glancing back once to brush her with his eyes. From across the expanse of the lobby, Rae felt the tangible touch of his eyes as though they were his hands roving over her body.

In the elevator, she leaned against the wall, her legs weak, her heartbeat fast. She couldn't rid herself of the lingering stamp of ownership with which he seemed to have branded her. She could even now visualize his dark features sculpted with a rugged hand. They were engraved in her mind with a searing permanency she doubted she could ever forget, even when he finally did leave Hamilton Oil for good. His impression of authority and quiet strength would be a lasting one, and now she was becoming even more enmeshed in his life.

Chapter Eight

Rae stood before her full-length mirror critically appraising the third dress she had put on. This was so out of character for her. She never fussed over what to wear, but nothing seemed to convey what she was feeling. Most of her clothes were simple and tailored for the office. She had few dresses to begin with; her usual attire consisted of suits or pants for the field.

A frown lined her forehead as she gazed at her reflection in the mirror. It would have to do, she decided, turning away from the picture of herself in an emerald-colored sundress that didn't quite create the soft effect she desired.

Against her better judgment she had been looking forward to this date with Jonathan. It was foolhardy, she had repeatedly told herself, but for some reason she needed to see a male appreciation for her in his eyes. He had left earlier than planned for Dallas because of some unexpected business, and she missed his bantering, teasing, shrewd sharpness which constantly challenged her.

When her doorbell rang, she wasn't ready. Her hair was still pinned up from when she had taken a bath and she only had half her makeup on.

The doorbell sounded again and Rae rushed to answer it. "Sorry. I'm not ready yet."

Surprise flashed in Jonathan's eyes while a roguish grin teased the corners of his mouth. "*You*, not ready! What's the world coming to?"

Suppressed laughter just under the surface, he walked into her apartment and made himself at home. Dressed in a white knit shirt and navy-blue pants, he was overwhelmingly handsome. The shirt revealed his broad, muscular chest, while the white contrasted perfectly with his tanned body.

Rae hadn't realized she was boldly staring at him until she noticed his amused expression. Quickly she closed the door and headed for her bedroom, trying to ignore his low chuckle but not quite succeeding.

Five minutes later she was finally ready, her hair now in soft curls that framed her face in an auburn cloud and her makeup accentuating her large gray eyes.

Jonathan stood when she reentered the living room, a very male glint in his dark eyes.

Let's forget about the party, she clearly read in his look.

Swallowing hard, Rae moved toward the front door. "We'd better be going or we'll be late."

"Heaven forbid!"

"How was Dallas and your mother's birthday party?" Rae asked, closing her front door behind her.

"A disaster." His face held a totally serious expression as he helped her into his car.

"What happened?" Rae asked when Jonathan was settled in behind the wheel.

"You weren't there." He flashed her a rakish smile that completely charmed her.

For a full minute she didn't say anything, not sure whether he was serious or just teasing.

"How was everything at the office? Any problems?"

"You'll have to wait until Monday morning, Jonathan King. Remember, no mixing of business and pleasure, and if I understood you, this afternoon is strictly pleasure."

"Yes, ma'am. I'll try and keep that in mind." He glanced at her, laughter gleaming in his eyes. "Have I created a monster?"

"No. My life is so wrapped up in Hamilton Oil, though, that it's nice to have a reason to forget it for a short time."

"Rae, you don't need a reason. There are more things in life than work. You have to create a balance between work and your personal life."

"I know. My father didn't and look what happened to him."

A lump lodged in her throat when she thought of her father's driving need to work. And what had he had in the end? *A daughter who felt left out of his life. A wife who had died, neglected and brokenhearted. A company that was now being run by someone else other than family.*

Silence reigned in the car; they were both deep in their own thoughts. His words kept repeating themselves in Rae's mind. What did she do other than work? She read a little, but she was usually too tired even to do that. Occasionally she played a game of tennis, but not in the last six months. And she hadn't been out to the ranch to ride since her father's death.

Jonathan stopped the car in front of Bradley's three-story mansion, built as if it were in the deep South on a plantation before the Civil War. The silence was becoming strained as he stared straight ahead, his grip on the steering wheel tightening.

Rae shifted in the seat, then blurted out, "It's certainly beautiful weather for a lawn party. Bradley couldn't have picked a nicer June day." What a thing to say! She laughed silently at the idea of sitting a foot from someone like Jonathan discussing the weather.

"Rae, I wish you wouldn't push yourself so much."

The concern in his voice touched her like a

velvet shroud. She felt insulated from the world as she met his gaze. She instantly thought back to her father's funeral when Jonathan had first appeared in her life. His concern then had trapped her in a silken cage, and she felt that same feeling now.

"You're the reason I'm pushing myself. *I want Hamilton Oil back.*"

"Don't lay the blame at my feet, Rae. We both know if I hadn't been here you would still be pushing yourself to learn everything about the company. At least I'm helping to cut some corners."

"And you think I should be grateful. Well, Mr. King, I'm sorry I haven't properly thanked you." Her crisp tone negated the meaning of her words.

"I'm not looking for your thanks. I'm protecting my own investment."

A parking attendant strolled toward Jonathan's car, sharply reminding Rae where they were.

In a weary voice she said, "No business today, Jonathan." All her anger drained away. It had been a long week, full of work and problems, and she truly didn't want this day to be marred. "Please."

He loosened his grip on the steering wheel, any hint of anger erased from his expression. "We don't seem to be able to separate the two very well."

"No, but we can keep trying."

"I guess there's always hope." Jonathan removed the keys from the ignition out of habit and climbed out of the car.

"What did your mother think of the porcelain figure?" Rae stood as the parking attendant took the keys to Jonathan's Mercedes.

She looked around at the expensive cars lined up to be parked and knew many of Tulsa's prominent citizens would be attending Bradley Fairchild's lawn party, held on his estate south of the city. She hooked her arm through Jonathan's, the anger of moments before forgotten as she anticipated an afternoon in Jonathan's company.

"She loved it, of course. I think that's the first gift I've given my mother that I don't doubt she really liked. I'll have to solicit your help at Christmastime and her next birthday."

Rae had no intention of being involved with him a year from now. That would really complicate a life she was struggling to keep simple. The worst part of this whole affair was that one moment she was elated to be with him and the next she was wary. This constant warring with herself was wearing her down.

Bradley's garden was breathtaking with its array of flowers arranged around a pool fed at one end by a waterfall. There was a bridge to an island in the middle of the pool where a bar was set up.

As Rae strolled along a path bordered by red tea roses, she acknowledged with a smile a few acquaintances and business associates.

"Do you want anything to drink?" Jonathan asked, his hand casually covering hers.

"A whiskey sour."

"And I'll have some champagne, brother

dear." Carole stood in front of them, dressed in a soft, flowing creation of chiffon that emphasized all her womanly curves.

When Jonathan left, muttering something about the fact that he didn't have three hands, Carole's laughter rang and her smile grew. "I do exasperate my brother with my wonderful timing."

A warmth emanated from Carole that captured a person's interest. Carole liked people, and Rae couldn't resist the silent signals of friendship Jonathan's sister was sending her. Rae realized it was another link in the chain that bound her to Jonathan.

"Maybe I should take lessons from you on how to get under your brother's skin."

"I certainly make Jonathan's life exciting. When I'm in town he can't say his life is dull."

"I doubt he knows what the word 'dull' means. The energy that man generates is astonishing."

"You shouldn't be taking lessons from me, Rae. It should be the other way around. I'm a thorn in Jonathan's side, but you're something entirely different."

"A whole sticker bush?" Laughter trickled through Rae's voice.

"You're different, Rae. He doesn't brush you aside as I've seen him do with other women. He had a comfortable relationship with a woman in Dallas for two years until the week he returned from Tulsa. Now, Victoria is seeing another man and Jonathan spends most of his time in Tulsa."

"Making my life miserable," Rae interjected.

"You're protesting too strongly. I think Jonathan's intrigued by you because you're the first woman who has stood up to him over and over again." Carole's eyes strayed to Jonathan at the bar, then hardened into two chips of amber as they returned to Rae. "Jonathan likes to control. Be careful, Rae. I don't want to see you get hurt. May I call you one day for lunch?"

"Yes, I'd like that."

"Maybe I can learn some ways to run my life more successfully. I must admit I've made my share of mistakes—"

"Just make sure those mistakes don't get back to Mother," Jonathan interrupted, balancing three drinks in his hands.

"I have you to see to that, brother dear," Carole retorted in a flippant voice, grinning mischievously before taking her champagne and adding, "See you two later. Got to keep Bradley in line."

Rae watched Carole stroll toward a group of men and flirt outrageously with them. Rae was beginning to feel Carole did a better job at handling Jonathan than she ever could. Carole loved her brother, but she didn't seek his approval or his love. Rae's eyes widened in surprise at the direction of her thoughts. *Love? That's impossible!*

Carole's warning replayed in Rae's mind. *Jonathan likes to control. Be careful, Rae.* That she intended to do; falling in love with

Jonathan King wasn't in her plans for the future.

"Bradley certainly has his hands full with her. I guess he knows what he's getting into." Jonathan handed Rae her drink, smiling in amusement. "In fact, I think my sister has met her match in Bradley."

Rae saw the source of Jonathan's amusement. Bradley was next to Carole with an arm clamped around her waist, murmuring his apologies to the men as he guided her away from them.

"Who do you think will win in the end?" Rae asked as Carole threw her an impish grin before turning a pout on Bradley.

"Bradley, of course."

"Why 'of course'?"

"Because I know my sister. She wants a man to dominate, to not let her get away with things."

"Maybe you only want to think that about her. Most people don't like to be told what to do."

"Most people or just you? It's been my experience that people don't want to take full responsibility for their lives and therefore their mistakes. Lots of people like the responsibility to fall on someone else's shoulders."

"Like yours?" she taunted.

"Yes, Rae, like mine. There are leaders in this world and followers."

"And you've made it quite clear that there can only be one leader at Hamilton Oil." Rae took a swallow of her drink to dampen the fires of her rising anger. Jonathan King knew how to make her mad. And he knew how to please her, her rebellious side reminded her.

"I'm not replying to that statement on the grounds that this is a gorgeous Sunday and I have a date with a beautiful woman with whom I would really like to be alone. Want a grand tour?"

The suggestive tone in his voice was undermining her reserve. She knew she should say no, that they would end up alone somewhere in Bradley's three-story mansion, but she didn't.

Twenty minutes later, after seeing most of the ground floor, Rae and Jonathan were alone in the library, the sun streaming through the large glass windows that overlooked the east and south sides of the lawn.

"I knew if I searched long enough, I would find an empty room," Jonathan whispered close to her, his breath tickling her neck under her right ear.

He didn't touch her, but his male presence was working to erode any resistance she might have. She had the impulse to lean into his strength, but she didn't. Instead she stood looking out the window, rigid, with her arms folded across her chest. Her skin tingled with the anticipation of his touch.

"Now that I've put in an appearance, let's leave." Jonathan's husky voice caressed her like a soft summer's breeze.

Rae turned, stepping away from him. "This isn't alone enough for you?" She wanted her voice to be light and casual, but instead it quavered.

"No." They were now only inches apart. "Those large windows look out onto the world. Most of our time together is spent with groups of people or at the office. Suddenly I don't want to share you with the world."

For breathless moments Rae lost herself in the intensity of his black eyes, bottomless pools of darkness. He vibrated with raw masculinity as he stood close to her, so close that his male scent draped her with a warmth that was deliciously exhilarating. His dynamic appearance ignited a primitive chord within her and she reached up to brush back a strand of toasty-brown hair from his forehead.

His dark eyes were now focused on her mouth with a reserve-shattering look that made her throat dry. She ran her tongue over her lips to moisten them.

"Oh, Rae, don't do that here."

She frowned, puzzled. "Do what?"

"Lick those sensual lips. You test a man's limits in a place where nothing can be done."

He traced her lips with a trembling hand while his gaze was trained on her eyes, watching for her reaction. The feel of his fingers on her mouth sent a melting current swirling through her, and this time she didn't fight the impulse to lean into him.

At first hesitantly, then with crushing force, he pressed her to his lean male frame, his face buried in her auburn hair.

"Oh, Rae," he moaned, squeezing her even closer.

The sound of people laughing drew them

apart, but the desire in Jonathan's eyes was evident even as the door to the library was opened by Carole and Bradley.

"I see you two beat us to it. I guess we'll have to find someplace else to talk," Carole said, but she was obviously in no hurry to leave.

"Yes, I guess you do," Jonathan drawled, slowly concealing his passion.

Suddenly Rae was roused from her languorous state and said, "No. We were just leaving." Things were getting out of hand. She definitely needed some fresh air!

"Sorry, brother dear. Looks like you'll have to try again later," Carole teased.

"I doubt seriously you're sorry about much of anything, Carole." Jonathan clasped Rae's upper arm and guided her to the door. "Good luck, Bradley. You'll need it."

Rae was quickly ushered from the room. The obstinate set of Jonathan's jaw spoke of his battle to retain control. But instead of going back out into the garden, Jonathan steered Rae to his parked car, not waiting for the parking attendant to bring it around to the front doors.

The ride to her apartment seemed to take forever. When he finally parked his car next to hers, he faced her, his smile slow in coming.

"I think my sister's one goal in life is to make mine as difficult as possible. Normally I don't let her get to me like this, but do you know what holding you does to me?"

Rae's heart was beating at such a fast rate

that she thought it would burst. The sensuous look in his eyes telegraphed his undeniable passion.

"Would you like to come in for some coffee?" Rae hadn't realized she was going to ask until the words were spoken.

"I thought you were never going to ask."

"I wasn't."

"That hit dead center. I don't know if my pride is going to survive knowing you."

"Look, Jonathan, I want to be truthful with you. That's the only way I can operate. I'm confused where you're concerned. I don't usually have this problem, but with you all my rules have been broken." Rae looked him squarely in the eye. "Since it's clear we will be working together for quite a while, we should try to be friends, but beyond that I don't think it would be wise."

"I get your message loud and clear, Rae. Nothing will happen between us that you don't want. Will that put your mind at rest?"

She placed her hand on the door handle. "The offer for coffee still stands."

"Are you sure?"

"I realize if we are going to be friends I need to get to know you outside the office."

"In that case I accept."

Inside her apartment it didn't take long for Rae to put the coffee on to percolate. She was glad she had something to do with her hands, which were trembling slightly from her speech in the car. Her mind had delivered that speech while her heart had protested.

"Can I help?" Jonathan asked from the doorway to the kitchen.

"No. It's all done," she said, hastily assembling the scattered pieces of her cool poise.

Friends. That's all, her mind reconfirmed.

If you say so, but I warn you it won't be easy, her heart responded.

"Good. I've put on a record. I notice we like the same music."

Thank goodness it was still daylight outside and the room was bright with sunlight, or she would have suspected he was deliberately setting the stage for a seduction scene.

Rae sat across from Jonathan, silent seconds stretching into silent minutes as they stared at each other. The soft music seeping into her soul was the only sound in the room.

A smile broke Jonathan's neutral expression, and he laughed deep in his throat. The pure sensuality of his laughter heightened the fine-honed paranoia that held Rae motionless.

"We could talk about the weather as openers, or do you think we have progressed further than that?" Jonathan's mouth, which could be hard and unrelenting or tender and devastating, curved into a wider smile.

"I think I've already exhausted the subject of the weather earlier today. How about the safe subject of—the Texas Rangers?"

"Are you a baseball fan?"

"No. I like soccer."

"Oh?" His brows arched in surprise. "I think we have more things in common than we ever imagined."

"You like soccer?"

"Don't sound so shocked."

"I would have thought football was more your type of game."

"Who said it isn't?" Jonathan moved from the chair he had been sitting in to the couch, his thigh dangerously close to hers. "A guy can enjoy more than one sport. I love football. In fact, I played on a team in college."

That didn't surprise her. He had the muscular build of a running back, coupled with the necessary quickness.

"I have an idea. The Tulsa soccer team is playing Thursday night. Come with me. I'll get two tickets to the match. They're playing the New York Cosmos. It should be an exciting game." The last sentence was added in a tenderly persuasive tone that further chipped away at her reserve. "Besides, what better place to get to know me than in the heat of cheering your team to victory against stiff competition? And one of the safest places is in a crowd of thirty thousand."

"I don't know if—"

"It's either that or a quaint, intimate dinner at my house. Which will it be?" His eyes twinkled with subdued laughter.

"What a choice!"

"You know which one I'm hoping you'll accept, Rae."

"The soccer match?"

"Hardly, but I'll settle for it if I have to."

"Okay, I'll go. The soccer match sounds—"

"Safe," Jonathan finished for her.

He took her head in his large hands and

slowly lowered his mouth to open over hers. She felt him shudder as he deepened the kiss, his tongue darting into her mouth like a dueling rapier.

He was slowly tearing down all her defenses, one by one, as the seconds were drawn out. Then, when she felt herself being imprisoned by his powerful but gentle assault, he pulled away.

"I'd better be going." His voice was rough, gritty, like sand over velvet.

He let himself out of her apartment. Rae sat on the couch, watching him leave, too stunned to respond. She squeezed her hands together to stop their trembling, but nothing could cease the lightning speed of her pulse.

Chapter Nine

"What's that?" Rae asked, rising from her chair behind her desk.

"Simple. A cart with food on it. You didn't think I would let you go to the soccer game without eating first, did you?" Jonathan tipped the boy who had wheeled in the cart, then began setting Rae's work table for dinner. "You can't cheer well on an empty stomach. Everyone knows that, Rae, and it's now six-thirty. The game starts at eight."

"Six-thirty! The last time I looked at my watch it was three."

"My, how time flies when you're having fun." There was a trace of sarcasm in his voice. He waved her toward the chair he had pulled out for her. "Come on. All of that can wait until tomorrow."

"I only have a few more things to finish. It won't take long." Rae sat down again and picked up her pen. "You go ahead without me."

She hadn't realized he had crossed the room until his hand closed around her wrist in an iron manacle. He took the pen from her hand and pulled her to her feet.

"No way, lady. This is *my* time now, not Hamilton Oil's."

"But—"

"No 'buts,' Rae Hamilton. I've been patient since five o'clock and I'm not always known for my patience. Now, come on and eat before these steaks get cold. We have to leave in forty-five minutes."

"Yes, sir. My, you're a demanding boss." As she was moving away from her desk, a white rose caught her attention and Rae placed a hand on Jonathan's arm to stop him. "Jonathan, the rosebud every day isn't necessary. What if people begin to talk?"

"I grant you the rose isn't a necessity, Rae, but *I* want you to have it. And I don't care what other people say." He grasped both of her hands, and the businesslike atmosphere completely evaporated with that one intimate gesture. "When I look at that rose, I think of you."

"But a fresh one every day? You don't even give the old one time to open up. What do you do with the day-old roses?"

"Throw them away. You're like that rose on the desk, closed to the world. One day you'll trust me and open yourself up to me."

His unwavering gaze burned her where it traveled and robbed Rae of the will to think coherently.

"Jonathan . . ." she whispered, the rest of the sentence forgotten as his hand stroked the column of her neck so lightly she wasn't sure he was even touching her. "Please, I . . ."

"Shh, baby. I've wanted to do this all week."

His mouth descended so slowly that she thought it would never claim hers. Impatiently she reduced the distance between them by pressing closer to him. His arms folded her tightly and tenderly against him, her body flattened against his solidness. The kiss began with a demanding urgency and ended with a searing appeal of sheer sensuality.

Parting slightly, his eyes soft, Jonathan studied her passion-drugged features. "I don't think two fans will be missed tonight."

Slowly common sense returned and she glanced around her office, vividly reminded of her resolve not to get in too deeply with Jonathan. Right now she felt as though she were drowning, and fought against that feeling.

"Oh, no. Every fan counts and especially against the Cosmos." Walking to the table, Rae began chatting to hide the sharp-edged tension running through her body. "You're right. I am hungry. Who wants to cheer on an empty stomach, and the hot dogs at the stadium aren't—"

"Rae!" Jonathan towered over her, hands clenched at his sides. "Enough! You've made your point. Let's eat."

She felt the strained atmosphere as if it were a palpable force. A fragile smile teased the edges of her lips as she looked into the intense absorption of his gaze.

"I keep forgetting you're not a patient man."

"I have moments when I can be very patient, Rae." The hard planes of his face gentled into a smile.

"I hope you remember that when you see my report on number two Carter."

His smile grew until a gust of laughter entirely dissipated the electrified tension. "I'll try."

They quickly ate their dinner, discussing the merits of both soccer teams. Rae was learning what an avid sports fan Jonathan was and that not only had he played football in college but soccer as well.

"When King Industries began requiring so much of my time, I had to give up playing for an amateur team."

"What do you do now to keep in shape?"

Rae vividly remembered the flatness of his stomach, the broadness of his chest and the sinewy leanness of his thighs. There was a muscled elegance about Jonathan which exuded a primitive sexuality. His body in motion was powerful, yet at the same time graceful.

"I swim whenever I can manage to grab an extra thirty minutes." Jonathan paused for a moment, a commanding countenance to his hard features. "Carole told me she had lunch with you today. What did you talk about for two hours?"

"Besides the fact the King family wants to make sure I get three square meals a day, it's none of your business."

"Carole is my business."

"Quit trying to be a domineering father to her!" Rae was looking directly into two black eyes, fierce and aggressively indignant.

An unbearable silence followed. "I see my sister has found a sympathetic ear in you." Jonathan sounded amused.

The husky appeal in his voice elicited an involuntary action—Rae's heart missed a beat. Relieved that the tension of a few minutes ago had faded, she sought a way to end this intimate dinner.

Jonathan captured her hand as she placed her napkin on the table; her senses reeled at the burning awareness of his touch. His male scent enveloped her while the stimulating caress of his hand on her arm danced along her nerve ends. She closed her eyes to savor the languorous warmth produced by his mere touch. Then suddenly he released her and a coldness swept over her.

"It's seven-fifteen, Rae. As it is, we'll have to park quite a ways from the stadium. We'd better be going or we'll spend most of the night walking."

Would that be so bad? Rae asked herself. *Strolling hand in hand with Jonathan on a beautiful June night with the stars shimmering . . .*

Fifteen minutes later Jonathan had parked his car on a side street over half a mile from the stadium. Taking her arm, Jonathan set a brisk pace that had Rae short of breath before they were halfway there.

"Hold it." Rae stopped dead in her tracks. "We have plenty of time before the opening play of the game."

He smiled sheepishly. "Sorry. Old habits die hard. I've always been a fast walker."

"Do you ever take nice, leisurely strolls?"

"Not many. Never had the desire or the time—until recently. But I doubt you do, either." He began walking again but much slower this time.

"Another thing we have in common?"

"Every day the list grows longer."

At the stadium they pushed their way through the large mass of people and found their seats as the two soccer teams were lining up. Throughout the game excitement charged the air. When there were only five minutes left, the Tulsa team was tied 1–1 with the Cosmos. A Tulsa striker had the ball and was driving toward the goal, dodging a defender with a well-executed maneuver. The striker shot and scored.

Rae was on her feet, throwing her arms around Jonathan. "We're ahead! Wasn't that a beautiful play!"

Their gazes locked. Jonathan's arms encircled her and suddenly Rae remembered they were in a huge crowd. Her arms dropped away and she tried to bring order back to her chaotic thoughts. Being in Jonathan's embrace for only a few seconds did strange things to her. It wasn't just the thrill of a close game that caused her heart to pound frantically against her breast.

People around her started to boo and hiss, and she noticed the teams weren't lining back up, which was what they should have been doing if the goal had counted.

"What happened?" Rae asked, craning her neck to see over the people standing in front of her.

"The referee called our team offsides. The goal doesn't count."

"That's absurd! They weren't offsides. What does our team have to do to win? That referee should have his eyes checked," Rae said in exasperation.

"If Tulsa doesn't do something soon it will go into overtime."

Jonathan regarded Rae with sparkling brown eyes. Even in the midst of over thirty thousand people he could make a situation seem intimate. Hurriedly Rae turned her full attention back to the game and concentrated even harder on cheering—anything to keep from dissolving into his arms again and completely forgetting where they were.

By the time the game was over, Rae's throat was sore from yelling so much, but she was too exhilarated to stop. The game had gone into a shoot-out and the Tulsa team had finally won. During the overtime and shoot-out both she and Jonathan had been on their feet most of the time.

They walked slowly back to Jonathan's car,

Rae's hand in his. "No reason to hurry. The traffic is going to be heavy for quite some time. I don't think anyone left the stadium early," Jonathan commented. A relaxed atmosphere prevailed between them.

"And that makes thirty-four thousand people all rushing for their cars at the same time," Rae said with a laugh.

Jonathan slipped his arm about her shoulder and drew her closer to him. They were heading down a side street, a canopy of tree branches overhead. The stars were glittering in a black velvet sky, the evening breeze soft and warm. Except for the fact that they were walking in the midst of a crowd all heading in the same direction, the setting was romantic.

Finally Rae and Jonathan were seated in his Mercedes, waiting to find an opening in the traffic. In irritation Jonathan turned off the engine.

"I might as well conserve the gas. We know how hard it is to find."

"And I thought you would bully your way into that line of cars."

"Not in this car. Besides, I like having you alone with me, sitting so close I can do this." Jonathan slid his arm about her shoulder and pulled her to him. "We'll wait it out. I'm in no hurry."

His mouth grazed a path from her neck across her cheek and teased the corners of her lips. She turned toward the warmth of his lips while his manipulating fingers kneaded the taut cords at the base of her neck. Fleetingly he brushed her lips, then captured the lower one between his teeth, nipping gently at it. She waited for his total possession.

The blare of a horn parted them, and they both looked at each other, then began laughing.

"I think the whole world is conspiring against me." Jonathan straightened and turned the key in the ignition, glancing across the seat at Rae.

His dark gaze blended with the blackness that surrounded them, but Rae knew what was in his eyes. The same thing that was in hers—a flaming desire which was becoming harder to control or to deny.

With his attention fixed on the traffic ahead, he said, "I've enjoyed tonight, Rae. I never pictured you as a woman who would yell or jump up and down when her team scored. Or tell the referee off when she thought he made a wrong call."

"That call was wrong and you agreed with me." She looked at him, his profile hinting at his amusement even in the semidarkness. "And how did you picture me?"

"Sitting there calmly watching the game with interest, but never so enthusiastically."

"That just goes to show that you don't know much about me."

"You're right there, but I'm certainly enjoying discovering what makes Rae Hamilton tick."

After Jonathan's chaste good-night kiss at her apartment door, Rae wandered into her bedroom totally bewildered. He was wearing her down, but for the life of her she couldn't seem to find an effective way to combat him or her traitorous body. There was a part of her that thrilled at his touch, basked in his attention and gloried in his kisses. If it were only him she had to fight, she would have no problem. *But how do I battle an alter libido that craves him in every sense of the word?*

By the time Rae left for the office the next morning, she wasn't sure how she was going to make it through the day with Jonathan so near. She had spent a restless night dreaming about him, but she was no closer to an answer to what she should do. Jonathan was deliberately eroding her composure with his passionate kisses, then his sudden withdrawal.

But throughout Friday Jonathan was all business, not a look or an accidental touch to remind Rae of the night before. It made working easier for her and she was grateful to him for that. But in the back of her mind, she was always wondering what his next move would be.

All day Saturday she was constantly on edge, waiting for his call or his sudden appearance at her door. He didn't appear, though, and Rae had to admit she was disappointed, if only because she had relished the idea of telling him she had other plans for the day.

Surveying her apartment the next day, she decided it never looked so clean. She had Jonathan to thank for that. The whole weekend she had worked cleaning and scrubbing to take her mind off him. But, of course, it hadn't worked. When she was scouring her bathtub, all she could think of was Jonathan touching her, leaving her wanting more from him than a few kisses. That made her even more determined to remain her own person. She would merely fight harder.

By Sunday afternoon she decided she had to get out of her apartment before she went stir crazy. She had reports to do but she didn't feel like doing any more work this weekend. Maybe lying out in the sun would help ease the tense feeling that had her all wound up.

It didn't take her long to gather up her swimsuit and head for her father's house. An hour later she lay stretched out on her back in a lounger by the pool, the sun warming her bikini-clad body, seeping into her and drawing out the tension. She liked to come over to the house to swim on the weekends since the pool at her apartment building was always crowded, especially with single men on the make.

A shadow fell across her and she lazily opened her eyes halfway. "What are you doing here?" she asked, her eyes flying wide open.

"I saw your car out front and thought I would stop by and say hello."

Jonathan sat in the lounger next to hers. He was dressed in navy-blue shorts and a beige knit shirt; she had never seen him so casually attired. This made him seem even more human. The powerful columns of thigh muscles, revealed by the shorts, drew her attention. Slowly she raised her gaze up his body past the width of his broad shoulders until it rested on his amused expression.

"Not everything I own is a three-piece business suit."

"I know that," she retorted in a harsher voice than she intended. But her stomach was fluttering and she didn't want it to.

"And I see not everything you own is for the office." His eyes slid appreciatively over her barely covered body, leaving a flaming path where they had been. He was deliberately ignoring her animosity. "I definitely approve, Rae. That bikini is very becoming on you."

Rae's first impulse was to snatch up her beach towel and wrap herself in it, but she decided instead to match his bold gesture with one of her own. Her study of him was one of such female interest that all amusement fled his expression and only desire remained.

"I'd ask you to join me but I can see that you don't have a bathing suit, so . . ."

He started pulling his shirt off, saying, "I think I'll soak up some sun. There are ways of swimming without a bathing suit."

"Well, let me know how it turns out," Rae quipped, standing and grabbing for her terry-cloth coverup. "I have an apartment that needs to be cleaned."

He seized her hand. "Now, is that being a good hostess? Surely the dust will be there later. Stay—*please*—and I'll take you to the concert at Utica Square this evening."

"What makes you think I'd want to go to a concert?"

"Anything beats housecleaning." With a

gentle tug, she fell into his lap and his arms imprisoned her against him. "Have a heart, Rae. I hate to sunbathe alone."

"You haven't done so badly." Rae's fingers were splayed across his tanned chest as she tried to wedge some space between them.

"It doesn't take much, Rae."

And Rae knew he wasn't referring to getting a tan but to something much more alarming. "Well, then I suggest you let me get up so you can tan. I'm blocking the sun."

"Oh, I don't mind."

The sensual huskiness in his voice was crumbling her inner wall stone by stone. He nibbled her bare shoulders teasingly, lightly, while his arms held her powerless.

"Mmm. You taste salty."

"Well, in case you haven't noticed, it's hot out here." Rae finally wiggled free and towered over him.

"Yeah, unquestionably hot, babe."

His laughing eyes were riveted on her as she dragged air into her lungs. Since his arrival the temperature had risen at least ten degrees! The refreshing water of the pool beckoned. Turning away from the relaxed picture of Jonathan, his arms now crossed behind his head, Rae dove into the water and began swimming laps.

At least in the pool she was safe. It would probably be a good idea to stay in until he grew tired and left. Exhausted from swimming twenty laps, Rae lay on her back and floated, completely relaxed now as the sun beat down upon her and the cool water enveloped her. The contrast was what she had needed.

A firm clasp around her ankle pulled her under. She came up gasping for air. Standing in chest-high water not three feet away was Jonathan, his laughter rumbling deep in his chest.

"I couldn't resist," he said, trying to contain his laughter.

Rae treaded water, forming a plan of revenge, then discarding it when she thought of a better one. Willing her mouth into a smile, she swam toward him.

"Don't even think it, Rae. You'll lose. I'm much stronger."

She stopped, suddenly alert, her eyes wide. He was naked! "Jonathan King!"

His laughter returned. "The servants are gone and this is a private pool. There's just you and me, babe. I couldn't resist your delectable sight lying so peacefully in the water. You were so sure I wouldn't come in and you felt safe."

"Why didn't you at least leave your shorts on?"

"Because we are going to the concert in an hour. Does my attire bother you?"

"Not one bit." She moved backward toward the steps.

"Where are you going, Rae?"

"To get dressed. If we're going in an hour, I need to dry my hair."

"Afraid," he challenged, a mocking gleam in his midnight-dark eyes.

"Of you?"

He nodded.

"Yes!"

Rae quickly climbed out of the pool before he tried to change her mind. She saw his clothes on the lounger and fleetingly thought of taking them. She glanced over her shoulder to watch him swimming laps, his powerful body, beautifully proportioned, slicing through the water, a perfect machine. An impish grin removed all doubt. Gathering up her clothes and his, she hurried across the lawn. She didn't bother changing at the house, but instead climbed into her car and directed it toward her apartment. She would have loved to see his expression when he discovered his clothes were gone.

When she reached her apartment, she quickly changed and was heading for the door to leave when the pounding began.

"I know you're in there, Rae Hamilton. Open this door before I create a scene *you'll* regret."

The thunder in Jonathan's voice held her motionless. How in the world had she thought she could get away before he found her? It was just that the picture of his clothes on the lounger had been too tempting for her to resist. She had never done anything like this before and she wondered again about her out-of-character behavior.

"Rae!"

Hesitantly she walked to her door, put the chain on, then opened it a crack.

"Yes? May I help you?" Was that her voice speaking so calmly?

"Open this door!"

"No! Not until you cool down."

Rae's gaze traveled downward. He was wearing a white terrycloth towel that barely covered him.

"If you don't open this door, I'll kick it in. No small chain will stop me."

The ominous smoothness in his voice now alarmed her even more. If it were humanly possible, he would carry out his threat. Slowly she removed the chain and stepped back.

The door slammed open and Jonathan stood braced in the doorway, features carved in cold marble. With deliberate slowness, he advanced into her apartment, kicking the door closed behind him, the sound reverberating throughout the room.

"Jonathan, stay where you are." Rae winced at the weak thread in her voice. Panic constricted her voice and she froze.

His pitch-dark eyes burned into the depths of her being with relentless fury. "What did you think you were going to accomplish by doing that? Embarrass me? Get me thrown in jail?" His voice vibrated with power.

Rae took a sharp breath and tried to assemble her scattered thoughts. His strong lines were so aggressively masculine, the hardness of his mouth so faintly cynical, that her mind was continually sidetracked.

"I didn't think . . . I just acted on impulse," she finally admitted while the beating of her heart hammered in her ears.

Again he moved forward, stalking her. She backed away until the wall stopped her. As each step brought him closer, Rae consciously arranged her features into a brave expression while her legs threatened to give way.

"If you had said anything else, I think I would have wrung your pretty little neck, Rae Hamilton."

A lazy hint of a smile edged the corners of his mouth as he melted her slender frame to his dominant strength. Her mind swirled with his erotic nearness. His distinct scent was like an aphrodisiac, prompting her senses to take flight, to soar to heights unknown to her before now.

"Do you know a few months ago I don't think you would have done anything so impulsive—or radical, Rae."

Rae leaned away to look him in the eye. "You aren't angry anymore?"

"I must admit I was at first, especially when I had to break into your pool house for this towel. But now . . ." He shrugged. "It's hard to stay mad at you when you look so delightfully beautiful."

His mouth possessed hers and became a driving coercion, parting her lips to let the sensual probe of his tongue incite her senses with his yearning petition. Winding her arms around his neck, she responded to the provocative enticement of his kiss with her own wild intensity, shocking one corner of her sensible mind.

He dragged his mouth from hers, his ragged breathing rasping in her ear as he whispered, "Get my clothes. If we want to make that concert, I'd better take a shower and dress."

Jonathan set her a good foot from him, a shutter descending over his features that made it impossible to read what he was thinking. She couldn't have misread his male arousal.

Seeing her dismay, Jonathan took Rae's face in his hands, compelling her to look at him. "*When* we make love again, it will be the perfect moment. You'll want me so much there will be no doubts flying around in that pretty head of yours. I want all of you, Rae, when we make love. *All.*"

The vehemence in his dark eyes bored into her and she was speechless.

When, not if. That disturbed her, but not nearly as much as the idea she was beginning to feel that he knew her better than she knew herself. It was as if he knew of the war of emotions battling in her but also the outcome. If so, that meant there would be more to this relationship than friendship. Her excitement was only outweighed by her fear.

Chapter Ten

$\mathcal{R}$ae watched Jonathan speaking to the group of investors as he presented the largest investment program Hamilton Oil had ever proposed. His dynamic presence commanded attention and each investor had a rapt expression on his face.

One part of Rae was learning, assessing his techniques for holding the audience's attention, his delivery of the program. But the other part of her couldn't keep her mind on the business meeting at hand.

Beyond Jonathan the skyline of New York was thrusting upward. Late last night they had arrived in the city for a series of meetings with their largest investors. Jonathan, George and she had worked on this proposal for months.

A shrewd question was directed at Jonathan and his face registered serious concentration. There were times his face was an impenetrable mask of dark features, and then there were times she clearly saw the desire for her in his expression, especially these last two weeks since the concert.

Lately she had been barely able to control her impulses to lace her fingers through his hair and haul him to her—right in the middle of his office in front of the other employees! And when he casually touched her she would grow hot and cold at the same time. But at all times he had been a perfect gentleman, not even kissing her once since that evening. Either he was a man of steel or a very experienced game-player, only marking time with her before he moved on.

A prickly sensation flashed up her spine and she looked from the window toward Jonathan. The midnight-dark force of his gaze seemed to weld itself to the gray of her eyes as he finished his presentation. He directed a frown exclusively at her, and Rae knew he was aware of her total lack of concentration on his presentation.

Later after the meeting, Jonathan took her arm in a bruising hold as he escorted her from the conference room. "If you want Hamilton Oil so badly, then I suggest you listen and learn," he whispered curtly.

For two weeks he hadn't spoken one harsh word to her, but it all seemed to be unleashed in that one sentence. She pulled from his grasp and retorted, "My, you place a lot of value on your expertise. I have sat in on my father's presentations before."

"How many, Rae? Do you want to make the next one?"

At the elevator she turned on him. "Yes! Yes! Yes!" she answered through gritted teeth, then pivoted and headed for the stairs.

Descending the three flights of stairs, she was strangely disappointed he had let her walk away so easily. But when she reached the ground floor and opened the door to the lobby, there stood Jonathan with a scowl on his face. She stopped, struck by his absorbing look, and waited for his next move.

The stubborn set of his jaw gave way to a crooked half smile as he extended his hand. "A truce?"

His fingers folded around hers and she murmured, "Yes."

"Good, because I have plans for tonight and I wouldn't want there to be any strain between us." Outside Jonathan hailed a taxi, then continued when they were settled in the back seat, "I have two tickets to see the play everyone's talking about and reservations for dinner at Maxwell's Plum afterward."

"Drop me off then at Fifth Avenue and Forty-eighth Street. I'm going shopping and I'll see you later."

One eyebrow quirked upward. "Shopping?"

"Yes. I feel like celebrating. You may not think I was paying attention, but I have a feeling we'll have no trouble getting the money we need for our new program."

"Woman's intuition?"

"If you want to call it that." But it was more the fact that she had supreme confidence in Jonathan's ability. In the last four months she had begrudgingly discovered he was a pro in the business world.

After depositing Rae at the corner of Fifth Avenue and Forty-eighth Street, Jonathan leaned back in the taxi and closed his eyes. It wouldn't take too much longer before Rae could run Hamilton Oil effectively. At times she was too conservative, but she was quickly grasping the financial aspects of the business. *Then why aren't I happier than this?* he asked himself, a depression cloaking him in a mantle of weariness.

Conservative wasn't the word Rae would use to describe the dress she had on. Daring, provocative, maybe—but certainly not conservative or businesslike.

The shimmering gold lamé gown, for which she had paid an exorbitant price today, clung to every curve as she moved toward their table at Maxwell's Plum. Two slits up each side revealed her long, shapely legs and the plunging neckline almost met her waist, hinting at her full, rounded breasts as did no other gown she owned.

It had taken a while to get used to the bold stares of men, but most of all to Jonathan's. He had been speechless when she'd opened the door to her hotel suite and for an instant passion had ignited between them, until he'd turned away and become the perfect gentleman again.

What had she wanted to prove with this gown? Rae wondered as she gave her order to the waiter. She was tired of all the games she and Jonathan were playing with each other. Things would be settled once and for all between them tonight. She wanted him to take her as he had that night at his house and she intended to show him tonight. With that purpose in mind she hurried them through dinner and was relieved when they had finally returned to their hotel and were riding the elevator to the tenth floor where their rooms were located next to each other.

At the door to her suite Rae handed him the key, saying, "Come in for a nightcap, Jonathan."

"Just one. It's been a long day and tomorrow with all those meetings scheduled will be even longer."

Rae indicated the couch as she made her way toward the bar. "A Scotch on the rocks?"

"That'll be fine." Jonathan slipped out of his dark blue coat, unbuttoned his vest and loosened his tie.

Looking at him with his feet propped up on the coffee table, Rae was barely able to pour the scotch. Her desire for him flamed to life, as though fireworks were exploding inside her. With a great effort she stilled the trembling within her as she placed his drink in his hand and sat next to him on the couch, her thigh brushing his on purpose.

Rae took several long sips of her wine. He had said she would have to make the next move and she wasn't sure how to start. Well, sitting here gulping down this drink as if it were water wasn't the answer, she decided.

Jonathan placed his empty glass on the coffee table and rose, bending to pick up his discarded coat. "I enjoyed this evening, Rae, but I have some work I need to do now." He started for the door.

"Don't go, Jonathan." She was on her feet and across the room before he had turned to look at her.

His gaze narrowed on her face. "Why shouldn't I?" he asked slowly, his expression unreadable.

"I want you, Jonathan. Please stay."

So low were her words that she wasn't sure he had heard her until he asked, "Are you sure, Rae? *Very sure?*"

"Yes, very sure."

Her arms stole about his neck and drew his head toward hers. Their mouths met and joined in a searing union that blazed a fiery streak through her.

"Oh, Rae, you don't know how long I've waited to hear that," he rasped into her ear before nibbling on her earlobe.

"And you don't know how long I've wanted to say that to you and couldn't get the courage up. I didn't know I was a coward until I met you." Laughter rang deep in her words. "But I'm learning to overcome that."

"That's the spirit."

Their gazes embraced and Rae knew that this evening was entirely in her hands. He would do *nothing* she didn't want.

She slipped her hands inside to remove his opened vest, then took off the tie. Slowly she unbuttoned his white silk shirt and slid it off his shoulders and down his arms. As it fell to the carpet Rae ran her fingertips over his broad chest, teasing him with her suggestive caresses. But he remained still with his arms at his sides.

She stepped away and pushed first one strap of her gown off her shoulder then the other. Both naked from the waist up, they stared deeply into each other's eyes for a long moment, silent messages transmitted between them.

Reaching out with one hand, Rae beckoned Jonathan toward her bedroom where she encircled him in her tight embrace, flattening her breasts against his hair-roughened chest. The sensation sent a renewed bolt of pleasure coursing through her and she clung fiercely to him.

When she finally pulled away she noticed the undisguised desire that flared in his dark eyes and his difficult breathing which spoke of the fragile rein he had on his passion.

But this was *her* night! Leisurely she unzipped her gown and stepped out of it, holding it away from her and letting it float to the floor. Then, at a tantalizingly slow pace, she removed first her nylon stockings, then her lace panties.

His quick intake of breath brought a smile to her lips as she boldly stood naked in front of him. There was no embarrassment as she approached him and undid his belt and trousers. With the same slow gestures, Rae undressed Jonathan while he intently watched her every action.

Even when they were completely nude, Jonathan didn't make a move to initiate anything. A taut thread ran through his tall, muscularly built frame as he regarded her through heavily veiled eyes, the only evidence of his restraint a sheen of sweat on his forehead. His arresting gaze made a swift, piercing study of her, then returned to inspect her face, waiting, always waiting.

Never before had Rae felt so powerful and daring as she led Jonathan to the queen-size bed. She gently nudged him onto the bed, then lay beside him.

"Be gentle with me, baby. I'm all yours." His voice was a slow, lazy drawl, pitched to a low, seductive level. The way he was looking at her made her feel as though he were making love to her in his mind, but that would be all if she didn't do anything else.

Running her tongue maddeningly slowly over her dry lips, she made an unhurried descent toward his mouth. All her senses reacted to his vibrant male strength as their lips greeted each other. Rae parted his lips with her tongue, and his mouth opened to receive her, her tongue now seeking the soft inside of his mouth and exploring it.

He groaned and she felt his trembling response, thrilling her and urging her to become even bolder.

"You're incredibly beautiful," she breathed into his ear before biting lovingly on his earlobe. His sheer male beauty provoked a sharp awareness in her, a quivering pressure taking hold of her inner core and spreading rapidly outward.

"Are you feeding me a line, Rae Hamilton? I won't submit that easily."

"You don't believe in my sincerity? Well, Jonathan King, I'll just have to show you what you do to me."

The testing exploration of her lips was replaced with a more demanding hunger which promised a flaming passion. She was really beginning to enjoy this aggressive role she was playing.

Her hands and mouth sought his secret places with a ravenous need to know him intimately, to be a part of him fully and absolutely. She gloried in the hard strength of his muscles, in the taut flatness of his stomach and in the muscular power of his thighs. She taunted him with teasing flicks of her tongue on his male nipples, the hypersensitive flesh of his neck and earlobe.

A low moan escaped him and for the first time his hands began to roam over her heated skin, caressing, squeezing, inviting more. Shuddering from the explosive pleasure that seized her, Rae had to end this sweet torment. She eased herself on top of him, finally bursting apart in a wild eruption of overwhelming fire.

Afterward Jonathan nestled Rae to him while she marveled at her total lack of inhibition. She had always prided herself on her controlled emotions, but strangely, she wasn't upset by the lack of it a few moments ago.

Jonathan disengaged himself and started to get up.

"What's wrong?" Her joy was quickly vanishing and apprehension taking over.

"I'm going back to my room." With his back to her, Jonathan was standing and stepping into his pants.

No! He can't be going now! Not after what we have shared!

"I thought you would stay the night," Rae said.

Facing her, Jonathan buttoned his shirt. "I have work to do before the meeting tomorrow morning."

Can't you do it tomorrow morning before the meeting? she wanted to ask, desperation resulting from a rising insecurity. *Hold me. Stay and reassure me I did the right thing tonight.*

But Rae didn't say any of those things. Instead she watched as Jonathan gathered up the rest of his clothes, kissed her briefly on the lips and left, telling her to bolt the door after him.

She spent the rest of the night tossing and turning or prowling her hotel suite. She observed the sun rise over the skyscrapers. But still, after berating herself all night for her behavior, she would have done it over again even knowing the outcome ahead of time. For a brief second she wondered if she was in love with Jonathan King.

"But if this is the way you're supposed to feel—miserable—then I'm surprised people ever manage to fall in love," she murmured as she prepared to join Jonathan for the meeting with the investors.

When she saw him, she knew he was worried about the new program. It meant a lot to Hamilton Oil—therefore him.

She should have been surprised that she was allowing her personal life to override her business life, but nothing surprised her anymore about herself. The fact that she was more worried about her relationship with Jonathan than any kind of new program with the investors seemed totally reasonable. She was changing inside, her feelings altering.

Somehow Rae made it through the meetings and back to her hotel suite, more exhausted from the turmoil her life was in than the long, tiring series of conferences. They would know soon enough whether the investors would go with their new program. All she wanted to do was soak in a hot tub, then sleep for twelve hours.

She had finished her soothing bath and was dressed only in a robe when she heard the knock at the door. A frown clouded her features as she went to answer it. She didn't want to see anyone tonight, especially Jonathan.

But there he stood, leaning against her door frame with a bottle of champagne in his hand and the most enticing smile on his face.

Moving past her into the living room of her suite, he said, "It's time to celebrate, Rae Hamilton. We got every penny we needed for our new program."

"We did! I knew it!" She threw her arms around his neck, excitement bright on her face.

"Yes, so you said. You must have some sixth sense about these things. I sat up most of the night doing some refiguring." His dark eyes blazed into her with a relentless zeal. "That wasn't what I wanted to do, but I had no choice."

"The man who is telling me all the time not to work so hard actually put work before—pleasure," she teased, suddenly happy. He hadn't left because he didn't want to be with her but because of his sense of duty. He had told her that last night, but she had been afraid to believe him.

He framed her face and stared intently into her eyes. "Rae, when I leave Hamilton Oil I want to leave it bigger and better than it was."

"Why?" Seriousness touched her features. "Why is that so important to you?"

"I'm not sure. Maybe it's because I liked your father. I like you. All I know is I must."

She stiffened. "Is that your natural protective instinct for the women in your life coming out again?"

"Do you consider yourself a woman in my life?" Jonathan asked in a deadly quiet voice.

Rae looked away from the probing depths of his black eyes. "After what I did last night, what do you think?"

"I know what I think, Rae. I want to know how you feel."

Her attention swerved back to his face and her breath caught at the sensuous look on it. "Yes!"

His hands dropped away and he pulled her against his rock-hard chest. She listened to his rapid heartbeat which equaled the fast pace of hers.

"I can't change how I am, Rae. I want to protect you, but I also admire your fierce sense of independence."

All the tension that had been building up since he had walked out of her suite last night faded. Instead, tingling sensations began to uncurl in the pit of her stomach.

"I want to finish what we started last night, baby." Jonathan swept her up into his arms and carried her into the bedroom, where he settled her in the middle of the bed. "But tonight it's my turn."

Quickly he discarded his clothes, then knelt beside her, unbelting her robe. The sides fell open to expose her naked body to his gaze, an extraordinarily gentle smile in his eyes.

"Do you know when I finally went to sleep last night all I did was dream about you? Rae Hamilton, you have bewitched me. What am I going to do?"

Rae wanted to answer, "Love me," but Jonathan brought his lips down on hers with demanding fire, investigating the inner sweetness of her mouth where her tongue greeted his in an answering caress.

His practiced lips knew how to arouse her, to dazzle her senses until she felt she would never think another rational thought again. She hadn't realized it was possible to be consumed by the mastery of Jonathan's masculine prowess, but she was.

Her passion was as unrestrained as his, having no limits as each explored the other. His kisses were haunting, tantalizing, teasing as they caressed her toward a dizzying height.

He pleasured her, delighted her, giving all of himself with each touch on her flaming body and each kiss on her sensitive skin. He enveloped her, absorbed her, seduced her, seeking the very core of her being and branding her his.

And she answered him with her own fierce appeal, wanting every ounce of him as hers. She matched him with her own intensity, each stroke, each kiss wildly frenzied.

For a short span of time they came together on a high plateau, joined as one, both giving all and taking all.

Rae fell asleep in Jonathan's arms, marveling that it felt very natural for her. A few times during the night she awoke, reassuring herself that Jonathan was still next to her. Then, nestling closer to him, his body heat transfused into her and she surrendered herself to the world of her sensuous dreams with Jonathan the only star.

Something grazed her cheek, tickling it, the sensation whispering through her dream-saturated mind. Slowly she regained consciousness and opened her eyes halfway. She encountered Jonathan's passion-packed expression. He was propped up on one elbow, lightly brushing her cheek with a fingertip.

As she surfaced from her languid sleep, a smile of sheer joy radiated her features. She stretched her arms above her head, then brought them around his neck, urging him toward her. His mouth drove into hers with a claim as strong and aggressive as the man himself.

He rubbed his mouth over hers, his voice rough with desire as he said, "I could make love to you all day long *and* all night long. You're a tigress, baby, that I alone want to tame."

His mouth ground into hers again with possessive firmness, his arms molding her to his naked contours.

"But, my little one, I want to show you New York. I have a feeling you've been here many times and have seen nothing of the city except conference rooms and restaurants. There is a lot more to New York than that."

"Could we negotiate a compromise?" she purred in a seductive voice she never knew she had until now. Her fingers roved the hard planes of his face, gentled with his passion.

"I think you'd have an unfair advantage over me. What do you have in mind?"

"This."

Rae kissed him boldly, her hands roaming over the taut muscles of his back then lower, pressing him to her.

"We could do both," she murmured against his lips before trailing feather-soft kisses down his neck and across his shoulder.

"Woman, you're a person after my own heart. The tour of Greenwich Village can wait."

It was two hours later before Rae and Jonathan were ready to leave the hotel, catching a taxi to Washington Square where they began their walking tour of the Village, Rae's hand securely settled within his.

After lunch in a quaint restaurant on MacDougal Street, Jonathan insisted upon taking Rae to the Metropolitan Museum. They explored the many rooms of the famous museum on Fifth Avenue until Rae sank onto a stone bench in the Sackler Wing, took her shoes off and rubbed her aching feet.

"I don't think I can walk another foot. I think I'll stay here and stare at this Egyptian temple while you finish the museum by yourself."

"No way. Besides, I must confess my feet are killing me, too. How about going back to the hotel and soaking our tired bodies in a hot bath?"

"Together?"

"That's the only way to take a bath."

"There isn't a tub in the hotel that would accommodate the both of us."

"Well, then we'll just have to compromise, Rae. You can take a bath first and I'll scrub your back, then you can scrub mine while I bathe."

"Do you think we've started something this weekend?"

"What?" Black firelight shone in Jonathan's eyes.

"All this compromising might catch on."

"Who knows? It has its possibilities." While Rae was putting her sandals back on, Jonathan continued laughingly, "Now, tomorrow we must see the World Trade Center, the United Nations, Lincoln Center . . ."

Chapter Eleven

"Good morning, Miss Hamilton. Is that a new dress? It suits you," Mrs. Daniels said as Rae walked into her outer office, a bright smile on her face.

"Thank you," Rae murmured, a blush staining her cheeks.

Inside her private office, Rae leaned against the door. Mrs. Daniels's comment hadn't been the only one she had received since returning from New York. Shane had teased her about wearing dresses instead of her usual tailored suits. So what if she chose to wear dresses occasionally? Women did all the time, even to the office.

Rae's gaze moved to her desk and her blush deepened. Sitting boldly in sight for everyone to see was a fully blossomed red rose. Every day this week there had been one on her desk, and she felt like that red rose, nurtured tenderly until she had bloomed and experienced complete fulfillment in Jonathan's care.

This time last week she had been sitting miserably through a series of meetings, berating her conduct with Jonathan the night before. Then her whole world had changed on Friday night. Friday night had been followed by Saturday night and Sunday night. They had postponed returning to Tulsa for two glorious days, while they discovered New York by day and explored the depths of their hidden passion by night.

Is this what it feels like to be in love? Rae wondered, but didn't know the answer. If she were in love with Jonathan, it gave him a lot of power over her, and she wasn't sure she wanted him to have that much control. She wasn't sure she should trust his motives and she didn't know how he felt about her. Love had never been mentioned this past week. She didn't fully understand what was happening to her, but for once she wasn't going to analyze and dissect her emotions.

For two hours Rae met first with Shane and then with George, knowing Jonathan wouldn't be free to see her until ten-thirty. But it was imperative that she see him then. Jonathan wanted to invest too heavily in a program with another oil company; she felt Hamilton Oil would be overextended.

He will listen to me now, Rae thought confidently. Not only did Jonathan have power over her, but she was finding she had power over him. Thinking back to the wild abandonment they both had felt when making love last weekend, she knew their relationship was totally changed from a week ago. She had felt a part of him, as though she belonged to him, and instinctively she sensed he had felt the same way.

Surely now he would listen to her and see her side of the issues. She didn't feel the program warranted that much of Hamilton's money, and after the failure of the sidetrack on number one McIntosh, she would make sure he listened to her opinion. Glancing at her watch Rae noted it was ten-thirty. With a quick look at the red rose, she decided it was time to present her arguments. Her heart was beating too fast and she had to admit she was afraid of what he would say. What Jonathan's attitude would be toward her professional opinions meant a lot more to her than she cared to acknowledge. Was she fooling herself into thinking things had *really* changed? They had for her, but what about for him?

With determination in the taut lines of her body, Rae headed for the connecting door to his office, knocked once and entered. For a few seconds she allowed herself the joy of drinking in the chiseled ruggedness of his bronzed features—that commanding jaw, the sensual mouth and those seductive dark eyes.

"Good morning, Rae." His gaze slid over her, noting the kelly-green silk dress that fell to right below her knees in soft folds. "That dress is so much nicer to look at than those suits."

His sexy tone of voice aroused her as if he were holding her in his arms and raining kisses all over her face. With merely one look he could send shivers down her spine.

But right now she was determined to keep this meeting on a purely business level. So far this week they had managed to separate their business and pleasure hours. The more she was around Jonathan, however, the harder it was becoming.

She advanced into his office and sat in front of his desk. "How did your conference go this morning?"

He tipped back his head and let his laughter roll from his throat. "In other words, no compliments between eight and five."

"Someone told me you were intelligent and I'm beginning to think he was right," Rae retorted, but a smile took any sting out of the words. "I want to discuss that investment program with Four Star."

"Don't you want to hear about my conference?"

The teasing light in his eyes made Rae even more resolved to keep their discussion on a serious level. She was becoming too tempted to give in to his bantering mood and completely forget about the investment program.

"No."

"I didn't think so. Okay. What about the program? I thought my report explained everything."

"Oh, it did. I don't have any questions about the program."

"Good."

"But I do question the amount, Jonathan. Now that we have to redrill number one McIntosh, since we lost the hole during *your* sidetrack when the drill pipe twisted off and we couldn't fish it out, I don't think Hamilton has that kind of cash to invest at the moment." Rae paused, halfway expecting him to interrupt her; but he didn't, which was a good sign. "We have our own investment program, the largest we've ever had. Don't you think it would be better to at least wait six months to see what happens with our program or invest half the amount you propose? I don't want us to run into a cash flow problem." That was so easy to do in the oil industry and Rae was determined it wouldn't happen again to Hamilton. The last time her father had had to bring in a silent partner.

Jonathan had leaned back in his chair with his elbows on its arms, his fingers forming a steeple. He was looking at her intently, deep in thought. Rae hadn't realized she was holding her breath until she was compelled to inhale deeply.

"I can understand your misgivings, Rae, but Hamilton Oil is going to invest in Four Star's program. It's a good opportunity to expand and I don't want to pass it up. Our cash situation is stable. We haven't spread ourselves too thin. I acknowledge we had some bad luck with number one McIntosh, but that's the only well we've missed on in quite some time. Hamilton Oil is on a roll."

"This isn't Las Vegas," Rae pointed out tartly.

"The oil business is a gamble."

Rae shot to her feet, distress whipping through her. "It's my future you're gambling with!"

It seemed as though they were back to square one. Who had she been kidding earlier? Nothing had really changed between them. In the business end of their relationship her opinion still didn't count to Jonathan. How could there ever be trust and hope of a lasting commitment between them if he constantly had to dominate and force his views on her? *I won't accept that!*

"I think you have made yourself quite clear, Mr. King. Good day." Gathering the fragments of her control about her, Rae left Jonathan's office, resisting the urge to slam the connecting door.

She walked straight to her desk, withdrew her purse and made her way from her office, telling Mrs. Daniels as she headed out the door that she would be gone for the rest of the day. It was time to take a well-deserved vacation; and it was time she visited the ranch and packed up her father's belongings.

Rae punched the "Down" button for the elevator with more force than intended, and winced from the sharp pain of a broken fingernail. *That's what you deserve, Rae Hamilton, for allowing Jonathan to get too close. I hope you've learned your lesson,* she told herself as she impatiently tapped her foot while waiting for the elevator.

When the elevator doors finally opened, she was a little calmer, her anger at Jonathan's domineering manner still there but more subdued. She greeted George with a half smile.

"Should I ask what's wrong, Rae?" George questioned, glancing sideways at her as he hit the "Door Close" button.

"Nothing a vacation, clean air and distance won't take care of. He can have Hamilton Oil!"

"I assume *he* is Jonathan King?"

George's quiet voice reminded Rae she wasn't alone and that it was unlike her to exhibit such anger in public. That was something else she had to thank Mr. Jonathan King for. She was losing control over her emotions, over her life. Damn him!

Instead of answering George, Rae smiled and said, "See you on Monday." Then she walked toward the front doors and outside into the fresh air. But the air wasn't cool. It was like a furnace—typical for a July day in Oklahoma. Quickly she sought the air-conditioned coolness of her car.

At her apartment Rae hurriedly began to pack for the two-hour trip to the ranch. She wanted to put as much distance between herself and Jonathan King as possible. She needed some time to think without his disturbing presence.

Her movements halted when the doorbell sounded. She thought of ignoring it, but she knew it was Jonathan and that he wouldn't give up until he saw her. She quickly placed the last piece of clothing in her bag and snapped it closed, then set it by her bedroom door.

Taking a calming breath, she thrust the front door open. "And to what do I owe the pleasure of this visit, Mr. King?" A coldness emanated from her, and she hoped it would freeze him. "Didn't you already make your point earlier today in your office? Over and over you have made it crystal clear who has the *only* say that counts in running Hamilton Oil."

She moved to shut the door, but his body blocked the defiant gesture. He pushed the door open with a quick movement of his arm and stepped into the apartment, kicking the door shut.

"So that's the reason you stormed out of the building."

"I hardly stormed, Mr. King."

"You're angry at me because I didn't take your advice on the Four Star program."

"You didn't even listen to me!" Her voice rose as she faced him with all her frustration and anger.

"I listened, Rae," came the quiet reply.

"Listened, then discarded."

"Listened, weighed the pros and cons, then decided against it."

His patience kindled her anger even more. "Well, thank you for at least weighing the pros and cons." Sarcasm oozed from every word.

He reached out to touch her, but Rae jerked away.

"Don't try that tactic on me."

"What tactic, Rae?" His own anger was evident in his clipped tone.

"Sex. You think by taking me into your arms and kissing me a few times, I'll be putty in your hands. It won't work, Jonathan King."

A hurt look crossed Jonathan's face and in order to retain her anger, Rae hardened the image of a predator in her mind. He had staked a claim on *her* company and had taken it. Now he wanted to do the same with her!

There was a strained tenseness to the silence between them, each eyeing the other. She waited almost as if she expected the air to shatter like a fragile vase.

His heavy sigh betrayed his bewilderment and troubled state. "Rae, we can't let our business relationship stand in the way of our personal lives. We started something beautiful last weekend in New York—"

"So I shouldn't act hastily and throw that *beautiful* relationship away. Is that the way you see it?"

Her interruption drew a cutting look of censure from him. "Maybe you'd find out how I see it if you'll let me tell you." There was a quality of quiet steel in his voice, a sharpness in his eyes as he regarded her.

"Okay. Explain." She impatiently brushed a strand of hair from her cheek, an indication of inner stress.

"Rae, something happened to us last weekend that I can't explain. I just feel it's important to the both of us. The emotions we experienced, I realize, are fragile, still tentative, but given time could develop into something lasting."

Her resolve wavered. This time Rae permitted Jonathan to pull her to him, embracing her against his granite strength. His hands began to weave a languorous spell as he bent and nibbled playfully at the shell of her ear, an action he knew could arouse her intensely.

"Rae, I hadn't intended to give you this until tomorrow night. I wanted us to go up to my cabin on Grand Lake, have a romantic dinner on the terrace, then make love all night long." Jonathan withdrew a jeweler's case from his front coat pocket and handed it to Rae.

She slowly opened the case, gasping when she saw the huge diamond pendant on a bed of black velvet. The large three-carat diamond caught the sun's rays and glittered. The cold stone chilled her.

Jonathan removed the pendant from its case and placed it around her neck; the diamond nestled between her breasts. Gathering her to him again, he kissed her deeply and thoroughly while Rae journeyed through a labyrinth of emotional uncertainty.

Rae fought the traitorous heat he was creating, realizing his attitude the whole week had been openly loving and subtly protective. There had also been a conviction as implacable as steel behind his every action. Again the realization that nothing had really changed battered at her.

She felt cheap. *Bought and paid for!* Shame engulfed her, and Rae rejected the sensual invasion of her mouth, twisting away from him in one swift movement. Fury raced like a scorching fire through her veins, in complete contrast to the coldness she felt at the touch of the diamond on the bare skin between her breasts.

Unclasping the pendant, Rae let it drop to the carpet. "Do you think this trinket will appease me? How little you know me."

She seethed in contempt, but he seemed unaffected by it. The air crackled with her intense emotions, while each measured the other. Finally in slow motion Jonathan bent and picked up the necklace, straightening and pinning Rae beneath his scornful gaze.

"You're right, I don't know you at all. I thought, after working with you for four months and spending what I had thought was a wonderful weekend, that I did. Obviously you were never taught to accept a gift graciously. I enjoy giving, but I can see you don't enjoy receiving."

The black depths of his eyes displayed the iron discipline that never seemed to desert him and the ruthlessly molded line of his jaw and mouth worried her more than she wanted to acknowledge.

The phone rang and Rae was relieved as she reached to answer it. She needed a break in the conversation to regain her poise and control.

"Yes, Shane?"

"I was concerned about you. You left without telling me you couldn't make our appointment for the afternoon. That's not like you. I need to see you about number one Jones."

"I'm sorry." Rae turned her back on Jonathan and continued in a low voice, "I'll see you in my office Monday at ten."

"We're off Monday because of the Fourth of July. Are you all right, Rae? You sound strange."

"I'm fine. Really. I just forgot about the holiday. Make it Tuesday at ten."

"Okay. See you on Tuesday, then."

When she turned back to face Jonathan again, her proud, aloof mask was securely in place. Suddenly she was glad that years of being her father's daughter had taught her how to hide her pain and feelings well. Jonathan had her so rattled that she had even forgotten about the Fourth of July weekend.

"I have nothing further to say to you. I want you to go now. My plans this weekend don't include you," Rae said.

"Going someplace?" His glance skipped from her suitcase, sitting in her bedroom doorway, to her. "With Shane?"

She thought of lying and saying yes, but she didn't want him or anyone to think she spent one weekend with one man and the next with another.

"Not that it's any of your business, but I'm going to my father's ranch where it's quiet and I don't have to answer to you." Tempering her voice to a lethal calm, she continued to talk as she strode to the front door. "Now, if you don't mind . . ."

Jonathan stalked toward her, his eyes like shards of ice. "But what if I do mind?" He ran a finger across her cheek and down her neck, his gaze fastened on the place the pendant had rested only moments before.

"I don't give a damn whether you do or not. Get out of my home—and my life, Jonathan King. You'll never own me and one day you'll get tired of Hamilton Oil and allow me to buy your shares back." She thrust open the door and stood aside.

"If you believe I'll give up this easily, then you don't know *me* very well."

"Do you want me to call the police? I mean to have you out of my life." Each word was a great effort of will, her anger escalating to explosion level.

"Good day, Rae. But not good-bye." Rage roughened his voice to a deep growl.

Later Jonathan wasn't sure how he made it to his house. He was so incensed he hardly remembered the streets he had passed or turning into his driveway. His death grip on the steering wheel loosened and he focused on his surroundings.

What in the world was wrong with the woman? If he had given that pendant to any of the women he had dated before, they would have been in his arms kissing him. The women in his life sought his protection and strength, whereas Rae seemed to scorn them.

Rae was so different from the women he had known in the past. Victoria, his mistress for the last two years, was the complete opposite of Rae. Was that why he had become bored with Victoria and had ended the relationship shortly after buying the controlling interest in Hamilton Oil?

Then there was his sister, Carole, who was always getting in trouble and begging for his help. And he couldn't forget that promise to his father to look after his mother for him.

Women! Jonathan tunneled his hand repeatedly through his hair, frustration screaming through his nerves. He didn't need Rae Hamilton!

That's a lie, King.

With long, angry strides Jonathan walked into his house, shutting the door with such force that the glass panes rattled. He needed a good, stiff drink to chase the image of Rae from his thoughts and to drown out the part of him that ached with his need for her.

Grabbing a Scotch bottle by its neck, he poured himself a tall glassfull. Maybe if he drank enough he would be able to forget last weekend; but he seriously doubted anything would help him.

Rae's skin had felt as smooth as cream and as soft as silk. Her kisses and whispered moans of pleasure had touched a part of him he hadn't known existed. And even now he couldn't forget the sensual smell of roses that was hers alone.

His hand slammed into the wood of the bar. But he was always doing the wrong thing with her. Why wouldn't she let him protect her, care for her? He suddenly realized that's what he wanted more than anything in the world.

If this was love, he was in for long, frustrating months, unless he could make her see his side of things. He did value her opinion. He had listened to her and had always taken her advice into consideration. Many times he had modified his plans because of her, but she chose to dwell on the times he hadn't budged from his stand. He'd wanted to make Hamilton Oil financially stronger this year and the only way was to strike boldly and intelligently.

Taking several sips of his Scotch, Jonathan weighed his options, something he always did when making a difficult decision. He could sit back and wait until she cooled off or he could go to the ranch and make *her listen to him.* He wasn't a man to wait when he could act instead.

With a single-minded purpose Jonathan was crossing the living room to leave for the Hamilton ranch when the phone rang. He started to ignore it, then decided it might be Rae, so he picked it up.

"Jonathan, I'm so glad you're home. I tried the office and they told me you had already left for the day." Carole paused briefly to catch her breath. "I'm in trouble. I need your help."

"Carole, that's not anything I haven't heard before. But this time you're going to have to get yourself out of the jam you're in. I'll always love you, but you're a big girl now. Solve your own problems. I have my own to worry about."

"But—"

"Good-bye, Carole."

Jonathan hung up and left the house, the phone ringing insistently in the background. He had never been that coldhearted before and he felt guilty now. But it was time he allowed Carole to grow up and stand on her own two feet without his continual support.

His laughter filled the silence in the car. Here he was wishing Carole would be independent of him and Rae would be dependent on him.

Make up your mind, King.

Chapter Twelve

*R*ae strolled from the barn where her father's quarter horses were still kept and let her gaze scan the open meadows around the ranch house. A wooded section in the distance bordered the shores of a lake, but she couldn't bring herself to ride out to where her father had died. In the past it had been one of her favorite places, but now she didn't care if she never saw it again.

Bittersweet memories flooded her mind. This ranch had been the only place her father could forget the pressures in his life and Hamilton Oil. But he hadn't come often enough to keep the worries and pressures from taking their toll on his health.

This had been one of the few places he had ever treated her like a daughter, instead of the son who was to inherit his vast empire. Thinking back over the years, she couldn't remember her father ever having told her that he loved her, and only on a few occasions had he hugged her—all at the ranch.

With a heavy sigh Rae began walking toward the house. She hadn't come here to relive memories, but to box up her father's papers and personal things. She had been at the ranch for over two hours and had postponed the task long enough. Once she was through she would relax and try to forget one Jonathan King, who disturbed her more than she cared to admit.

She didn't understand the man! Why did he feel she needed protecting? She had managed to care for herself all her life.

"Miss Rae, when do you want dinner? There's a square dance over at the Baileys tonight at seven," Slim said, stopping Rae's progress toward the main house.

Slim was a large man, at least a hundred pounds overweight. He was the cook for the ranch hands as well as for the guests.

Rae smiled at Slim's not-too-subtle way of saying "if you want to eat it has to be by six."

"Don't bother, Slim. I'll grab a sandwich later after I finish cleaning out Dad's study."

"I'm glad you're finally getting around to it. Nancy always hates to go into that room with all his things still out everywhere."

Rae started again for the house. Poor Nancy. She had been in love with Raymond Hamilton for years and her father had only seen her as the woman who came to clean the ranch house twice a week. But when they had stayed at the ranch, Nancy had always had an excuse to come to the house, usually to bring her father his favorite pie.

Her father had been so callous and unemotional that he had never taken time out to read between the lines. The cold, ruthless business world he had existed in had hardened his heart to ice. Rae cringed at the realization that life might hold the same fate for her.

Unanswered questions fragmented her thoughts, and her temples throbbed from the emotional stress she had been through since she had awakened this morning. *First Jonathan and now this*, Rae thought as she opened the door to her father's study.

The room was exactly the same as when her father had been alive. Papers were neatly stacked on his desk. Fishing trophies adorned the mantel over the fireplace and several large fish were mounted on the walls where there weren't any bookshelves. The room was actually a combination den/library. There were two couches near the fireplace and a sitting area in one corner of the spacious room where a television set was situated. Her father had never had time to watch TV in Tulsa, but he had spent a great deal of time watching his favorite shows or riding and fishing when he had been here at the ranch.

Dread slowed her steps across the room to Raymond Hamilton's desk. Rae would tackle the worst first and clear out his desk now.

She had finished boxing up the contents of two drawers when she turned to the long, shallow top drawer. Almost immediately her gaze flew to a ledger where her father had recorded the births, sales and deaths of all his quarter horses. Rae could remember one in particular that she had fallen in love with as a teenager and the anguish she had felt when the mare had died giving birth to a colt. She had just graduated from college and had come here for a short vacation before starting work at Hamilton Oil.

Absentmindedly Rae flipped to the page where her father would have recorded the mare's death and the colt's birth. Her attention froze on a stark white piece of paper. She closed her eyes for a brief moment, as if that gesture would dispel the paralyzing anxiety that for some reason clawed at her insides. Through the thin paper she had caught the words "My dearest daughter."

As though she were in a trance, Rae very carefully unfolded the white piece of paper and read.

My dearest daughter,

I'm not a man of words. In fact, in many ways I'm a coward, hence this letter instead of telling you to your face.

All those years you were growing up, I was wrong in demanding you be the son I never had. Your mother constantly told me that and probably that's why I kept insisting you be like a son. Pride can destroy a person quicker than anything, but it was impossible for me to change a bad habit overnight. I am an old dog set in his ways.

I never told you how much I love you but I do. I was so proud of you today when you graduated from the University of Oklahoma in the top of your class and informed me you wanted to come to work for Hamilton Oil. You're everything I could have ever wanted in a son. I'm extremely proud to call you my <u>daughter.</u>

Please don't judge me too harshly, and have some kind thoughts for your father.

> With all my love,
>
> Dad

"With all my love, Dad." The words echoed through Rae's mind, bombarding her over and over with the truth she had never known.

"Why didn't he ever tell me? Why didn't he at least give me the letter six years ago?" she whispered, her voice fiercer as the letter's contents struck her like a physical blow. "Oh, God, why couldn't you, Dad?"

Tears threatened, lodging in her throat and making each breath she inhaled difficult. Rae stared at the letter until her eyes ached, the words blurring together. With tears streaming down her cheeks, she wadded the paper, clutching it in her fist.

All those years wasted! She knew her father hadn't been a man of words. *But "I love you" isn't much to say,* she silently screamed. *Had it been that hard to express your real feelings, Dad?*

Rising slowly, Rae walked to the bay window and sat on the bench, drawing her knees up and hugging them to her. She laid her head on her knees and stared out the window, not seeing anything, the tears still scalding her face.

The shadows lengthened, but Rae barely acknowledged the passing of time. It hurt so much to finally know her father had really loved her. She had fought so hard for his love and respect and had always felt she had fallen short of both.

Am I turning into someone like my father, incapable of showing any deep emotions?

Too numb to even answer her own question, Rae shut her eyes, her thoughts splintered, barely held together. She became insulated in a dark void where no emotions were allowed to enter, no thoughts were permitted to form. Reality was forbidden.

From afar Rae heard the door to the study opening, but her head felt so heavy that she didn't bother to lift it to see who had entered. Nothing really mattered anyway. She felt so empty inside, as though all her emotions had vanished completely the moment she had read her father's letter.

"Rae?"

Jonathan's strong hand grasped her shoulder, a comfortably pleasant feeling, but Rae tensed beneath the touch.

"Rae, please tell me what's wrong." He sat

down next to her on the cushioned bench and with a firm lift of her chin, compelled her to look at him. "Please, baby."

Renewed tears crowded her eyes at his incredibly gentle voice and the infinitely tender expression in his dark eyes. She blinked and tears coursed down her cheeks to drop onto his hand. His hand quivered as he touched her cheek where her tears left a wet trail.

Many times she had silently cried for some show of tenderness from her father and here was a man she had fought tooth and nail with giving it to her.

"Don't cry, baby."

Jonathan gathered Rae to him, her pain transmitted to him. If only he could absorb it all for her, he thought, feeling utterly helpless. Listening to her cry against him, he desperately wished he could soothe away the hurt forever. His chest felt crushed, as if each breath he dragged into his lungs wasn't enough to sustain his life. *Oh, dear God, let me help her.*

"Rae, please tell me what happened. Honey, please don't shut me out."

It seemed an eternity before she quieted, a time when Jonathan's helplessness grew and threatened to overwhelm him. Her distress became a part of him, affecting him as though it were his own.

At first he hadn't understood what she was saying. Her words were mumbled against his shirt. But when she unclenched her hand and held up a wadded piece of paper, he knew she wanted him to read it. A parade of emotions flickered across his face as he read the letter—rage, sympathy and finally a glimpse of understanding.

"Do you want to talk about it, Rae? Sometimes it helps." He wanted to touch her, make love to her, but right now he knew she needed to talk, if she would. Something that festered in you for this long could destroy you if you didn't get it out in the open.

Rae twisted about and gazed out the window, her voice low, devoid of emotions. "For all the years I can remember, I lived in the shadow of my father's disappointment that I wasn't a boy. Do you know that until I went to college and majored in engineering my father and I never spoke more than polite words to each other? Until I came to work at Hamilton Oil, we never had a *real* conversation. Oh, he didn't totally ignore me. I received gifts on the appropriate occasions and his attention from time to time when he wasn't busy working."

Rae wiped at the tears, now drying on her cheeks, anger conveyed in the gesture. "Strangely, though, I understand my father. You see, I'm a carbon copy of him. He was dead inside unless he was working. His whole life was Hamilton Oil and he was only alive when he was there."

Finally Rae looked at Jonathan, the pain in her voice mirrored in her gray eyes. "But I don't want to be like that. He wrote his feelings down on this piece of paper but he never gave it to me. He couldn't even do that. Once he had expressed them, it had been enough for him. *But it hadn't been for me!*" She crushed the letter in her hand and threw it toward the fireplace.

"Shh, baby. Believe me, you aren't at all like your father. When I think of last weekend, you're more alive than most women will ever be."

Jonathan cradled Rae tightly to him, his hand stroking her back until finally the tenseness flowed from her and she relaxed within the tenderness of his arms. The even beating of his heart produced a calming effect, his gently whispered words the sedative she needed. Seconds fused into minutes and Rae's fragile emotional state grew stronger.

Jonathan took her hand and pulled Rae to her feet. "Let's go for a walk. I think we could both use some fresh air."

She settled her hand more comfortably in his, as though making sure her link with him was secure. "We could ride."

"Nope. I'm afraid not."

"Why?"

"I can't ride a horse and I don't intend to learn at this late date."

"You can't ride!" Her eyes widened in surprise. "You've lived all your life in Texas and Oklahoma and you can't ride?"

"Correction. I've lived in big cities like Dallas and Tulsa all my life. Now, are you going to show me the ranch?"

"We'll take the jeep since you can't ride."

At the study door Jonathan paused, placing

his thumb under her chin and tilting up her head. "All right?"

"Better. Thank you," she murmured.

"Spend the weekend with me. I want to get to know you, Rae. I've handled our relationship all wrong. Part of the reason is because you're different from the women I've known. I'm just beginning to understand the differences and why they are there."

Fear crept into her eyes.

"No, don't turn away from me. Give me a chance. Please. I want to prove to you that you can feel very deeply. I want to prove to you there can be more than work and Hamilton Oil in your life. During these few months after your father's sudden death, you've felt lost and overwhelmed. Now is the time to get a perspective on your life."

The fear faded in Rae's eyes. "Is that an order, boss?" A smile crossed her expression.

"No, a request from a friend."

A primitive longing welled up inside of Rae, and she couldn't have said no even if she had wanted to. She needed to believe everything he was telling her, but she had shut off her emotions from herself and the world for such a long time. She wasn't sure that Jonathan would even be able to penetrate her heart.

"Does that mean for the weekend we are on equal footing?"

He eyed her with suspicion. "More or less."

"Which, more or less? I like to go into a conference knowing where I stand."

Amusement was etched deeply into his features. "Well, I've tried my best to dominate and run your life and you keep resisting me. So I guess I have to try it your way—at least for the weekend."

"Oh, that long!"

"Woman, I'm not used to making so many sacrifices." As they walked toward the front door, he draped an arm about her shoulder and pulled her close.

"There always has to be a first time for everything."

"Why? I like the way my life is." *King, do you really? Let's face it. You were bored when you came to Tulsa. Rae has definitely added a spark to your life. But you're scared to admit that, my friend.*

Under Rae's direction Jonathan drove the jeep over the dirt roads that crisscrossed the Hamilton ranch. For an hour Rae avoided the lake area, then suddenly she decided that she had to face it sooner or later. She sensed it would be easier with Jonathan by her side. His presence was the balm she had needed earlier to get a grip on herself. The shock of reading the letter was finally wearing off and a rush of feelings was swamping her, all centered on Jonathan King.

When he brought the jeep to a stop at the lakeside, he twisted sideways to look at her. "I'm sorry about the pendant. It wasn't meant as a bribe or as an insult. I saw it and simply thought of you wearing it with that gold lamé gown you bought in New York. I couldn't pass it up." *Actually, King, why don't you tell her*

*the whole truth? You envisioned her wearing
it with nothing on.*

"You were right. I'm not used to receiving
gifts like that."

"Rae, you have to understand. I *enjoy* buying gifts for my woman. What's the use of
working hard if you can't spend your money
the way you want?"

My woman! Was she his woman? Strange,
those possessive words didn't upset her one
bit. They would have three months ago, but
not now.

"And another thing you must understand,
Rae. I can separate my business life from my
personal life. But I'm not sure you can. My
rejection of your opinion this morning was in
no way a rejection of you and what we shared
last weekend."

Rae stiffened, quickly moving from the
jeep. How dare he accuse her of not keeping
the two separate! But hadn't she walked into
his office, confident he would listen and obey
because of what had happened in New York?

Confusion shadowed her expression as she
stared across the water, imagining the place
where her father had fallen overboard. She
was sad, but the pain of his death was gone
now, as though his letter had erased those last
haunting memories that had been unresolved
at his death. Too late she knew of his love, but
those feelings of failure were replaced with a
new strength that released her from the past.
In her mind she was finally able to say good-
bye to her father.

Jonathan's hand clasped her upper arms and drew her back against him. "I had to say those things, Rae. I want there to be nothing between us this weekend. Not Hamilton Oil. Not our pasts. Not anything. We're just a man and a woman who desire each other. Nothing more."

His whispered words tantalized her neck, and a shiver of excitement rippled down the length of her.

"Are you sure that's possible, Jonathan? So much has already occurred that—"

He turned her to him and silenced her objection with the demands of his lips, his tongue plunging into the warm fragrance of her mouth, tasting, seeking, probing.

"No, I'm not sure, but then if we don't try, we won't ever know for sure. Come with me to my cabin on Grand Lake. We can be totally alone, isolated from the rest of the world."

"The ranch hands won't bother us here."

"No, but memories are associated with this place that could be a barrier between us."

Rae twisted around and indicated a spot near the middle of the small lake. "That's where my father was fishing when he had his heart attack. Do you know I had asked my dad if I could come up to the ranch that week after I checked on the Jones field? But he had insisted he needed me at the office. He had wanted a few days alone. He so rarely had any. But if I had been here maybe he wouldn't have died."

"Don't you dare feel guilty, Rae Hamilton!"

The emphatic, savage tone of his voice momentarily took Rae by surprise. Until now she hadn't realized she had subconsciously been feeling guilty. Jonathan was right, though. Her father would have gone fishing alone and she wouldn't have been able to prevent his death.

"Rae, you know your father gave you his supreme compliment. He left the care of Hamilton Oil in your hands."

"Actions and words are two different things. A person needs both to feel secure. But you're right. There are too many memories here for me to relax and enjoy this weekend. I'd like to see your cabin at Grand Lake."

Jonathan nuzzled her neck, feeling the strain of the last few moments seep out of her as she melted back against him. "Oh, baby. I know you've had to be independent, but lean on me a little. I want so much to protect and care for you."

"I don't know if I can, Jonathan. I've never been allowed to."

My Lord, what kind of childhood had Rae had? All Jonathan's instincts told him to proceed slowly, but it was hard not to hug her tightly to him and never let her go. How do you teach another person to put trust in you when it was something you weren't used to doing with others yourself? *with patience,* he cautioned himself.

For a long time Jonathan merely held Rae to him, his arms locked across her front, as though to shield her from any further pain.

She stared at the water, her breathing uneven, her body taut.

Then slowly Jonathan began to stroke the tension from her, his hands rubbing up and down her arms.

"Trust me, Rae. I don't ever want to hurt you, little one."

His soft words washed over her, stirring tingling sensations to life. Trust him? Could she? Should she? This man had the power to hurt her far more than her father had.

Turning within the circle of his embrace, she touched his beard-roughened jaw, reveling in the scratchy feel of it under her fingers. His dark eyes narrowed on her, a passionate intensity that Rae had never encountered in his expression, and she couldn't look away. Instead she became absorbed by the depth of the claim he was silently declaring to her. She basked in his rapt expression and found herself dissolving under the melting impact of his heated fervor.

Jonathan's hand trembled as he lifted it and explored the contours of her face. His thumb studied her mouth in detail, and a disturbing sensuality entered into his touch as he threaded his fingers through the silken tangles of her hair, holding her head firmly. Slowly his mouth drifted onto hers and his tongue mingled with hers, tentatively experimenting, then boldly investigating the recesses of her mouth.

Sighing moans of shuddering surrender escaped from her as his mouth transversed her neck, his hands unbuttoning and removing her blouse to expose the ripe fullness of her breasts. Her nipples responded, hardening under the fire of his gaze.

First he toyed with one nipple, brushing his fingers across it, then his attention turned fully to the other. Each touch drugged her with its erotic message and her breathing became labored. When his mouth followed where his fingers had been, she didn't think she would ever breathe properly again.

"Oh, Jonathan, I need you."

Words she had never uttered aloud before charged the air, and Jonathan brought his head up, the warm rapture in his eyes her undoing.

Her senses vibrated with her secret desire to shout, "The hell with Hamilton Oil! It's you I want." But years of keeping a tight rein on her emotions kept her quiet. The thought, though, filled her with a radiant glow of longing merely to be his woman.

His mouth feathered her cheek, moving in a blazing path toward her lips. He teased the corners of her mouth until she ended his taunting game and tasted fully of the warmth of his kiss.

Jonathan fitted Rae to him with one arm while he slid the other to the waistband of her jeans. Quickly he unsnapped her jeans and divested her of the garment.

His raw maleness was working on every one of her senses, her appetite hurriedly soaring to the fevered pitch of his. The exquisite ache in her loins insistently commanded he totally possess her now, this minute, but Jonathan seemed oblivious to her silent urges.

Finally, with a quickness evolving from a clamoring need, Jonathan undressed, then settled Rae on a bed of grass. His hands again traveled over every inch of her, weaving a magic with each whisper-light stroke. Rae arched beneath his touches, whimpering softly as a passion-filled tension mushroomed within and threatened to consume her.

She quaked as her slender frame met the hard planes of his body, his teeth nipping at her earlobe. His husky whispers—proclaiming her beauty, the satiny feel of her body, her sweet scent—incited her beyond this world, into a realm of the senses where everything became sharply focused on his hands, mouth, voice.

Then, somewhere in that other world, they met and clung desperately to each other in the tempest of completion.

Long moments later, cradled within his embrace, Rae rejoiced at what had just happened between them. *I love him!* That she knew now with unwavering certainty.

She nestled even closer, her fingers luxuriating in the hairs on his chest. The teasing suggestion of her fingers taunted his heated flesh.

His arms clasped her to him as he growled, "I *have* created a monster."

With a coquettish look she asked, "Are you too tired, Jonathan?"

"Are you crazy, woman? I'll never be too tired for this."

His mouth fastened onto hers with a swiftness that drove the breath from her. This time Rae expressed her newfound love with each caress, with each kiss.

Chapter Thirteen

You aren't going to make me do all the work? You have to carry your weight around here, too," Jonathan protested as he lifted a heavy box of groceries from his car.

"But I thought I was your guest. Guests aren't supposed to work." Rae stood next to his Mercedes and stretched her cramped muscles.

"Consider the game plan changed, then." Jonathan set his box down, took a bag of groceries from the car and placed it into Rae's arms.

The cabin was large, a house by most people's standards, with three bedrooms, two full bathrooms, a spacious living room and dining room combination and a kitchen most women would envy for all its modern conveniences.

Rae liked the rustic, cozy feeling of the place and knew this weekend would be special.

After they unloaded the car Jonathan collapsed into a chair in the living area, patting the armrest for Rae to sit on. "Would you like to go for a midnight swim?"

"You're right about it being midnight. Don't you ever get tired?" Rae asked with a laugh, enjoying the feel of Jonathan's arm about her.

"I can rest later. Maybe next week sometime."

"I thought we were going to relax. You aren't one of those people who comes to the lake and is on the go from minute one?"

"Let me show you how to relax. Come swimming. The lake will be refreshing after all that work you did unloading the car. Trust me."

There was that word again. She wanted to trust him, but her father had taught her to be cautious. It would take time to overcome her basic wariness.

It didn't take long to get into their bathing suits. Jonathan teasingly protested the use of the garments, but Rae overrode his objections. A lot of things were changing so quickly in her life that she was grasping onto a few old habits. She had never gone swimming without a bathing suit.

Bright outside lights lit the way down the steps to the dock area where Jonathan had a speedboat and a large platform on which to sunbathe and practice diving. Rae slipped off her coverup and peered over the side of the wooden platform.

"I think I'll let you go in first," Rae said. "I'm not sure I want to swim where I can't see the bottom. I think I'll moonbathe."

Laughing, Jonathan stalked her. "I wouldn't want you to get moonburned." He pinned her against the boathouse, his features shrouded in shadows.

"Well, in that case I'll go back up to the house. Where in the world you come off calling that place a cabin, I—"

"Be quiet, woman," he murmured right before his mouth crushed down on hers, cutting her off. Sweeping her up into his arms, Jonathan headed for the edge of the platform.

"Jonathan King, don't you even think it. I'll—"

Her protests were cut short as Jonathan unceremoniously dumped her into the lake. The cold water engulfed her and Rae struggled to the surface, an angry tirade hovering on her lips. But before she could say anything she was hauled against him, his laughter the only sound she was aware of.

"Oh, so you think that's funny. Are you harboring some secret desire to drown me? First in the pool and now here."

One of his arms secured her firmly to him while they both hung on to the ladder by the platform. "My desires are hardly secret where you're concerned."

Even in the cold lake she felt his male arousal and thrilled at the sensations of frigid water and hot passion. With deft fingers he unclasped her bikini top and tossed it up on the platform. Then his hand moved lower over her stomach to her bikini pants. He stroked her through the bottom half of her bikini with a maddeningly sensual skill. It wasn't long before she hated the idea of the material separating them.

"Please," she moaned, now clinging to the ladder, her body trembling with her desire.

Jonathan understood her all too well; his fingers slipped inside the fabric, caressing the now-moist core of her passion. It was Rae who removed the rest of her bathing suit and then worked Jonathan's loose.

Even with the cold water enveloping her, Rae was afire with her need for him. They melted together in the water, fiercely, savagely, their actions frenzied, uninhibited, as though all the primitive wildness had been unleashed in them.

Afterward, on a large towel atop the platform, secluded from the world, they took their time to enjoy each other; the urgency was gone, but the vehement desire to be close was as strong as ever. His hands and mouth began a new study of her soft, yielding body. He exploited every place that aroused her with the knowledge and skill of an expert.

She felt so helpless against the brushing caresses of his hands over her breasts, each nipple shrinking with stiff readiness. Then his mouth traced the same delightfully sensuous path, taunting her with his teeth.

The warm July air and the dark of night encased them in a sensual cocoon, causing each to be wonderfully attuned to the other.

His hands ended their poignant search of

her body and then it became her turn to excite him with her growing expertise. The savage onslaught of his mouth softened as he rolled over and positioned Rae on top of him, their lips never parting.

Her hands made their own examination of Jonathan's hard body, lean and strong. Deliberately, insolently, she tormented him with light, breathy caresses. The sweet torture she created sent tremors ripping through him as his arms tried to lock around her.

"No, Jonathan. Lie still. Not yet."

"How much more do you think I can take?" he demanded huskily.

"Your body is so magnificent. I want to know it as well as your mind."

"Isn't that the man's line?"

Ignoring his teasing question, Rae moved her fingers down his flat stomach to the muscled columns of his thighs, then leisurely upward again, finally touching his hot maleness.

"Oh, dear God, Rae," he groaned, and hugged her fiercely to him. "Class is over for the day."

The sheer intensity of his ardor silenced her doubts about the future. Everything would work out in the end. And no matter what happened, nothing would ever take this treasured night away from her.

"Time to get up, lazybones."

Jonathan's deep baritone voice sliced through the haze of sleep that clung to the corners of Rae's mind. She resisted his urgings, rolling away from the hand that was shaking her.

"Leave me alone," she moaned, pulling the covers up over her head.

"Not after I slaved away to make you breakfast." He gently slapped her on the bottom.

The action sent Rae bolting up in bed, her auburn hair tousled, an appealing sleepiness still shrouding her features as though she were remembering some provocative dream.

"Jonathan King! You're going to pay for that." Rae started to whip the sheet from her when she saw the tray sitting on the nightstand. "For me?"

"Who else?" Jonathan set the breakfast tray on her lap; a beautiful red rose in a vase lay next to a plate laden with delicious-smelling foods.

"This looks great. I've never had breakfast in bed." After spreading cherry jam on her buttered toast, Rae cut into her eggs and began to eat.

A few minutes later she glanced up and asked, "Where's your breakfast? Aren't you going to join me?"

"I've already eaten. I just want to sit here and enjoy watching you eat."

Feelings he had provoked within her the night before were reflected in his eyes, and Rae warmed under his regard.

"What are we going to do today, tour director?" she teased, remembering the weekend in New York and his "grand" tour of the city.

"A surprise. Finish up, then get dressed in your bathing suit. I have to check on a few things at the dock." Jonathan rose from the bed, kissed her on the top of the head and left.

Rae quickly ate the rest of the breakfast, deciding it was the best meal she had had in a long time. After dressing in her swim suit, she made her way down the stone stairs to the dock, where she found Jonathan preparing to use the motorboat.

"Are we going for a ride?" Rae asked.

"No. Skiing."

"I can't ski, Jonathan."

"You mean to tell me you've never gone skiing before? That's a crime, Rae. Look how many lakes there are around Tulsa. There's even one at your ranch." Jonathan untied the motorboat from the dock, then started the engines.

Over the noise Rae retorted, "I could say the same about you riding a horse. Look at all the horses in Oklahoma."

"Okay. I concede we've both neglected certain aspects of our education. But today we're going to change that. I'm teaching you how to ski."

"Not unless you let me give you some riding lessons."

He glanced over at her with a lazy look of wickedness. "I suppose there's no way I can get out of that?"

"Nope. Afraid?"

"Who? Me?"

"Yes, you, Jonathan King."

He motioned her closer. "I'll let you in on a secret no one knows. Horses and I don't get along."

"If your competitors ever found out you have a weakness, look out, Jonathan."

"But I know I can trust you to keep quiet," he drawled in a casual voice, but his eyes probed her intently.

Something unidentifiable passed between them. He could trust her because she would never do anything to hurt him. And she was beginning to feel she could trust him. After the profound tenderness they had shared last night, how could she think otherwise?

Jonathan cut the engine in the middle of the lake, saying, "Try the skis on and make sure they fit."

For the next ten minutes Rae listened to Jonathan's instructions. She didn't have any misgivings until she jumped overboard and he had started the engines. Clamping her hands around the wooden bar that was her link with the boat, she waited anxiously as the rope became taut.

"Okay, you can do this," she muttered to herself right before she felt the jerk of the boat speeding suddenly forward, and she was dragged five yards before remembering to let go of the rope.

"Let's try that again," Jonathan called out as he brought the boat near for her to grab hold of the rope.

"That's easy for you to say. You didn't swallow half the lake."

"Next time you feel yourself falling, let go *immediately*."

"Feel myself fall? I never got up to fall."

Rae quickly reached for the rope and this

time mentally prepared herself for the sudden force of the motor. She was ready for the yank on her arms and managed to rise out of the water to a squatting position for twenty feet before she lost her precarious balance and went flying forward, letting go of the rope the instant she struck the water.

Rae could see Jonathan was having a hard time containing his laughter. Fuming, she said in a too-sweet voice, "Don't get too smug, Jonathan. Wait until you see the horse I have picked out for you. Thundering Devil should be perfect. You two, I'm sure, will get along great."

"One more time?" His mouth was quivering, his eyes dancing with amusement.

"You're asking?"

"I just thought you might want to give up."

"You know me better than that. I'm not giving up now until *I ski*."

It was on the sixth attempt that Rae skied to a small cove and back before she motioned for Jonathan to slow down by the dock. Having let go of the rope, she gradually sank into the water, removed her skis and swam to the wooden platform. She barely made it up the ladder before she collapsed exhausted, her breathing labored.

Jonathan docked the motorboat and was beside her with concern in his voice. "You're all right, aren't you, babe?"

"My brain's alive but my body is having a hard time deciding."

"Maybe I could help it out."

His hand moved over her back, then grazed

down each leg, her body shivering with awareness.

"It's just been revitalized." Rae turned over, shielded her eyes and looked up into Jonathan's face.

"I want to make love to you right here in broad daylight, but I'm afraid we'd draw a crowd."

Jonathan's hands cupped her face and she turned to kiss a palm, then each fingertip.

"When I'm with you it's hard to think of the outside world, Jonathan."

"Do you hear what you're saying?"

"Yes. I haven't thought of Hamilton Oil once in twenty-four hours."

"That's got to be a record." Laughing, he scooped her up into his arms and started up the steps. "And I have a bottle of champagne in the refrigerator. Let's celebrate."

"Jonathan!" Rae punched at his shoulder. "I'm not that bad. You work as hard as I do."

"But as I've told you, I have a balance to my life, Rae. You've been single-minded, excluding everything and everyone." Jonathan set her down, tilting her chin up with his forefinger. "I take time out now to relax and to do the things I love to do. When was the last time you took a vacation?"

"I'm taking one now."

"You call one day a vacation! My Lord, woman, I've got a long road ahead of me. And the first thing we're going to do when we get back to Tulsa is clear up our work and fly to Grand Cayman for a week. I have a condominium there and I love to scuba dive. The water around the Cayman Islands is perfect for diving and I want to share it with you."

"But there's so much to—"

Placing his hand over her mouth, he ordered, "Not one word of protest. Remember, I'm still the boss and suddenly I feel the urge to do some—work on Grand Cayman."

Rae straightened to attention. "As you say, you're the boss. But I've got to warn you I don't know how to scuba dive, either."

"Somehow that doesn't surprise me. Come on. Let's open the champagne."

Jonathan was uncorking the bottle when the ring of the phone drew his attention. Cursing softly, he snatched up the receiver and growled, "Hello."

"Oh, Jonathan, I've been trying all morning to get you," Vanessa King cried over the phone.

"Calm down, Mother. What's wrong?"

"It's Carole. She's pregnant and wants to keep the baby! What are we going to do? She isn't married. Your father would be furious if he were alive. The scandal will be impossible to live down. My only daughter raising an illegitimate child. Oh, Jonathan . . ." Vanessa's voice became even more shrill, then quiet sobs took over and she couldn't finish her sentence.

Jonathan's features hardened into grim lines. What in the hell was he going to do now? His sister sure had a knack for getting herself into trouble.

"Mother, I'll be there as soon as possible. Please calm down. I'll talk some sense into Carole."

"Jonathan, I'm not in Dallas. I'm at the house in Tulsa. Carole's in her room here and she won't talk to anyone."

Jonathan's grip on the receiver was so tight the whitened skin was stretched tautly over his knuckles. Carole had never cared one bit if her actions hurt anyone else. Who was the father? Bradley?

Jonathan hung up, a rigid tension holding him motionless until finally Rae touched his arm and said, "Is Carole all right, Jonathan?"

Hard lips curled into an unamused smile, his hand raking through his brown hair. "It seems my sister went and got herself pregnant and wants to raise the child by herself." Cynicism was heavy in his voice as the travesty of a smile completely disappeared and Rae was pinned by his cold, calculating stare. "We'd better get going. I have an hysterical mother in Tulsa and a sister who needs some sense pounded into her."

Rae wanted to say something but the fury in Jonathan's forbidding look struck her speechless.

After packing hurriedly, they were on the road heading for Tulsa in less than fifteen minutes. The silence in the car was so unbearable that Rae would have loved to hammer her fists into his chest, anything to get a reaction from him, to crack the stern, stony expression on his face.

He hadn't said two words to her since they

had gotten into the car. She wanted to share this problem with him. She wanted to tell him not to barge into the house insisting Carole do things his way.

A silent question furrowed her brow when Jonathan pulled off the main road halfway to Tulsa and parked his Mercedes in front of a truck stop.

"Since it's after two and we haven't had lunch, I think we should grab something to eat now. I'll probably need my strength when I do finally see that sister of mine."

"What are you going to do?"

For a few seconds Rae thought he was going to reply, "None of your business."

Again a chilling smile slowly moved across his features. "I'm not going to do her physical harm, if that's what you mean." The palm of his hand slammed into the steering wheel. "But for the life of me, I don't understand Carole. To tell Mother first when Carole knows how fragile Mother's health is."

"If you start demanding that Carole do things your way, she'll walk out."

"Carole? She's always run to me to make things right for her. This time will be no different. She'll do as I say. She doesn't have any choice in the matter."

"I'm warning you, Jonathan. Don't be surprised if she doesn't. This is different from getting herself into some frivolous scrape. She's going to have someone's baby."

"You don't have to spell out the situation to me. I know the facts of life, Rae," he snapped.

"That's typical. You don't want any help.

229

You have to stand alone, King. Heaven forbid that you would stoop to taking advice, especially from a woman."

Rae yanked the door open and marched into the restaurant, stopping inside the door to get her bearings. The place was almost empty and after pausing a few seconds, she headed for a booth. Jonathan sat across from her, a scowl deepening the lines on his face.

"For the record, you hardly know my sister. So I don't see how you could be called an expert."

"Have you ever given Carole any credit? Have you ever given your sister a chance to grow up?"

"Don't try to place the blame of Carole's pregnancy on my shoulders. I won't accept that," Jonathan said harshly.

"I'm not. But your manner of handling her has something to do with it."

His black eyes drilled into her for a relentless moment before he said in a frosty voice, "Play psychologist somewhere else."

Throughout their lunch and for the rest of the trip to Tulsa, an oppressive silence prevailed. It was useless to talk to him, Rae decided as she stared out the car window at the quickly passing scenery. Did this weekend mean much to him? He had never spoken of love. In fact, right now he was the one who had retreated behind a wall and wouldn't let her near him. Maybe their outlook was too different for them to ever find a compromise. Could two such strong, proud people ever get together?

Chapter Fourteen

Jonathan brought his car to a sudden stop in front of his house, only a precarious hold on his temper. The rigid set of his shoulders, the hard, unyielding lines of his jaw and mouth worried Rae.

"Jonathan, please *listen* to what Carole has to say."

"And I've told you I know how to handle my sister."

"Have you ever thought that Carole's way of getting your attention was doing all those things? You were always there to come to her rescue, but did you spend much other time with her? How old is Carole?"

"Twenty-one," he answered in a clipped voice, his penetrating gaze fixed on her. "What's your point?"

"Your father has been dead for over thirteen years. You've been more of a father figure to Carole than he was. There's fifteen years separating you two. Not the usual age difference between brother and sister."

Climbing out of the car, Jonathan tossed over his shoulder, "I'm her brother, not her father."

With a deep sigh, Rae followed him into the house. He wasn't listening again.

Carole stood on the bottom step of the stairs, defiance engraved into her features, her hands on her hips. Rae offered her a faint smile, but Carole's attention was immediately commanded by Jonathan.

"What in the hell have you gone and done, Carole King?" he thundered, any rein on his temper entirely gone now.

"Shh. Mother's upstairs resting."

Jonathan strode to the stairs, anger in his every move. "And when did you care what Mother thought or how much you might hurt her? How could you tell her without talking to me first? You know Mother has had anxiety attacks before over things far less disastrous than her daughter getting pregnant without the benefit of a husband. Do you even know who the father is?"

Carole's eyes widened for a brief second, then she lifted her hand to slap Jonathan, but he caught her wrist in an iron hold.

"How could you say something like that to me? The father is Bradley, of course." With all her pride Carole tilted her chin a fraction, yanked her arm from his grip and whirled to head up the stairs.

Jonathan's hand clamped around her upper arm and he swung Carole back to face him. "We are going to talk *now*."

"You mean I'm going to listen to you rant and rave. No way. I'm sure Mother has heard us and is wondering what is going on down here."

"I'm overwhelmed by all your concern," Jonathan said sarcastically. "Rae, will you please look in on Mother for us while Carole and I have our little discussion?"

"Yes."

Rae was relieved to have something to do, but as she climbed the stairs, her apprehension surfaced; she had never met Jonathan's mother. What should she say to her, especially under these circumstances?

No one had bothered to tell her where Vanessa King's bedroom was, so Rae knocked on the first door near the staircase. When there was no answer she moved to the second door. From within the bedroom, she heard a faint voice. "Come in."

Rae hesitated for a long moment, listening to the quiet of the house. At least Carole and Jonathan weren't shouting at each other, but that didn't mean much. Jonathan's worst voice was his deadly quiet one, which could cut a person to the bone quicker than a cobra could strike.

Inhaling deeply, then releasing the breath slowly, Rae thrust the door open. Her eyes quickly adjusted to the dim light in the room, heavy velvet draperies shutting out the bright sunlight. Vanessa King sat propped up in bed with a washcloth over her eyes, looking every bit the frail woman Jonathan had said she was. His mother couldn't be more than five feet tall with iron-gray hair and delicate, porcelain features.

"Mrs. King, I'm Rae Hamilton, your son's— business partner." Rae had been about to say friend but after this afternoon she wasn't sure.

Vanessa removed the washcloth from her eyes, placed it on the nightstand, then rubbed her temples. "I suffer from severe headaches and I forgot my medicines in Dallas in my haste to get here. I hope Dr. Holifield will return my call soon." Her voice grew fainter, her eyes fluttering closed.

"Is there anything I can do?"

"I heard loud voices a moment ago. What is going on downstairs? Is Jonathan here?" Vanessa, with the same dark eyes as Jonathan's, was staring now at the foot of the bed. But there was none of the lively brightness in her eyes that there was in Jonathan's.

"Yes, Mrs. King." Rae sat in the chair next to the bed, glancing at the six perscription bottles on the nightstand.

"I must see him. He's got to make Carole understand what she will be doing if she keeps this baby without marrying." Vanessa's voice rose to a shrill level, her hands shaking. She clasped them together in her lap and looked straight at Rae. "Jonathan has always taken care of things before. He can't fail me now." Tears misted her eyes. "I don't know what I would have done after John's death if it hadn't been for Jonathan. Carole was only eight then and was going through a difficult stage. But I thought everything was fine with her now until she called me in Dallas early this morning. I . . ."

Tears rolled down Vanessa's cheeks, and Rae moved to the bed to comfort Jonathan's mother. Rae began to understand why Jonathan wanted to protect and care for all women. He had had to for so many years with his mother and sister that he didn't know any other way.

But Rae knew she would suffocate if he completely shielded her from the world and problems. She had heard once you shouldn't go into a relationship thinking you could change the other person. It rarely worked.

Finally Vanessa King composed herself and sat up straight, patting at her wet cheeks with a lace handkerchief.

"I'm sorry, Rae. I wouldn't have done that except Jonathan has talked so much about you that I feel I already know you."

"I don't mind, Mrs. King."

"Please, Vanessa. After I poured my woes out to you, I feel at least we should be on a first-name basis." A brief smile appeared on her mouth.

When the phone rang, Rae welcomed the break in the charged atmosphere. Apparently it was Dr. Holifield, since Vanessa was describing her symptoms.

During the last two days Rae's emotions had fluctuated like the weather often did in Oklahoma. One day it would be in the eighties and the next in the forties. Rae had gone from hot to cold to hot and now to lukewarm where her feelings concerning Jonathan were involved.

"Thank goodness Dr. Holifield finally called." Vanessa broke into Rae's thoughts. "He's sending over some medicine that should help." Jonathan's mother slumped back against the pillows, weariness aging her face, a pallor beneath her dark features. "I don't understand Carole. She's always been so good."

Jonathan had certainly done a great job of protecting his mother, but had he been fair to Carole? Rae wondered. Her father had always taught her to be responsible for her own actions. "You should take the blame for your own mistakes and the credit for your achievements," he had told her when she had first come to work at Hamilton Oil.

"Rae, I must talk with Jonathan." An urgency entered Vanessa's voice. "He's got to protect this family from a scandal."

"He's talking with Carole in the study right now."

"Good. Will you make sure he comes up to see me afterward?"

"I'll wait downstairs until they are through. Is there anything else I can do?"

"No. Just get Jonathan for me."

The desperate ring in Vanessa's voice saddened Rae. Suddenly she was glad her father had made her stand on her own two feet early in life.

Dread leadened Rae's steps down the hallway to the staircase. Had Jonathan listened to Carole's side? When his father had died, a lot had been placed on his shoulders by his family and business. His mother had wanted him, in fact had encouraged him, to take care of everything. By now it was quite natural for him to do things his own way. But Carole wasn't really like her mother and was now rebelling. Was Jonathan an immovable mountain? Rae wanted to be able to say no, but she couldn't. She didn't know.

Pausing at the bottom of the stairs, Rae glanced toward the study door. Muffled voices could be heard but there was still no shouting.

Rae prowled restlessly about the living room, the wait making her more tense as each minute passed with no indication of how things were going. She stopped in front of the mantel and stared up at a family portrait, painted at least fifteen years ago. Jonathan had a maturity even then about him, but the lines of experience weren't there. In the portrait there was still a boyish appeal in his features, his expression carefree.

Jonathan had told her he now had a balance between his work and play. Had it been a long, hard haul for him to achieve that? She sensed that at one time he had put his work before everything. How else would he have been able to expand his father's company tenfold in such a short time? Then he, of all people, ought to understand her driving need with Hamilton Oil.

After last night she had begun to feel less confused about what she wanted, but now the confusion had returned to plague her in full force. She and Jonathan were so much alike, and yet so very different.

The door to the study slammed open and Carole stormed from the room. At the front door, she turned on Jonathan, saying in a voice full of anger, "You can't make me do anything, brother dear. I'm twenty-one."

"I still control the money." Jonathan's voice was unusually quiet, almost a whisper.

"Do you think Mother would ever let me starve? Do you honestly think you would let your niece or nephew go hungry? I'm calling your bluff." Carole spun around, caught sight of Rae standing in the doorway of the living room, and added, "If you are smart, Rae, you will get as far away from my brother as I intend to." Then she yanked the front door open and left.

None of the tension in the atmosphere dissipated with Carole's departsure. Instead, it thickened the air with a stifling density. Apprehension made her shudder.

Without a word to her, Jonathan moved back into the study, and even though he hadn't closed the door, Rae felt he might as well have. His actions, though, cemented her determination to find out where things stood between them.

"I need to talk with you, Jonathan."

"Am I going to be subjected to one of your dressing downs?" A sardonic twist of the lips slanted across his arrogant features.

"I gather things didn't go well with Carole."

"You gather correctly."

Jonathan sat on the edge of his desk, his legs stretched out in front of him while his arms were folded across his chest. His casual, bland expression didn't fool Rae one bit. Underneath that neutral look lurked a leashed predator, waiting for the right moment to strike victoriously.

Rae treaded cautiously into the subject she wanted to discuss—their future, which was looking bleaker by the second. "Give Carole some time. If she just found out she's expecting, she's probably still trying to get used to it herself. It takes time for a person to adjust to a new situation."

"If I had wanted your opinion, I would have asked for it." The quiet retort warred with his unrelenting, steely regard of her. "It seems my sister admires you and the way you stand up to me."

"And what's so wrong with that?" Anger snapped to life in her gray eyes, intensifying their silvery brightness.

Jonathan surged to his feet in one fluid movement, the lines of his body taut, his senses alert. "A hell of a lot is wrong! My mother is upstairs with one of her headaches, no doubt. My sister won't listen to reason. And you're about ready to launch into a lecture on my sister, whom you hardly know."

"Jonathan, I fight for what I believe in and I don't ever want to change that."

His poise completely shattered. "Was that what you were doing this weekend?"

His rage struck her like fragmented shards of sharp glass. "What do you mean by that?"

"You believe in Hamilton Oil. It's your whole life and you have resented the hell out of me coming into that life and taking over the company. Was this weekend a new tactic to get me to let you run Hamilton Oil? If so, it won't work, Rae."

Rae bled from the invisible wounds of his accusations. A mixture of pain and fury threatened to take her breath away as she stood perfectly still, her face ashen, her mind churning with so many conflicting thoughts.

Swallowing hard to coat her parched throat, Rae silently counted to twenty, the normal number of ten not nearly enough to calm the rage that was building toward an explosion.

However, when she did finally speak, none of the control that she had wanted was evident. It was impossible to remain composed when she had seen her whole future destroyed in a few short minutes.

"Go to the devil, Jonathan King. You two have a lot in common. I had no intention of lecturing you on Carole, but since you have already condemned me for it, I might as well. *You are wrong!*"

Jonathan started to say something, his expression packed with all his fury.

"Don't you dare interrupt me, Jonathan. You have said some pretty nasty things that I have a right to answer."

None of the anger left his features, but he did lean back against the desk again, his body seemingly relaxed. However, there was an inflexible, obstinate set to his jaw and mouth.

"You have to let Carole be responsible for her own mistakes. You're partially responsible for this situation, because every time she got into trouble you jumped right in and took care of everything, as you've done for years. You can't live someone else's life. Most people have a hard enough time living their own. Who do you think you are that you can live everyone's life around you, making decisions as if you were a—*king*?"

"Have you had your little say?" A fire simmered in his black eyes.

"No! I came in here to discuss *our* future, but I can see there is no future to discuss. I *thought* we had shared a wonderful experience last night, but I should have known better than to believe in fairy-tale endings."

With pride deeply etched into her features, Rae pivoted and strode to the door. "Your mother wants to see you. Go to her. Good-bye, Jonathan. Go run someone else's life."

If she had thought there was a glimmer of hope for them to work things out, it had died completely by the time she was out the front door. Jonathan hadn't tried to stop her.

Jonathan's narrow gaze bored a hole into the carpet where Rae had stood only moments before.

Go after her, King. She's the best damn thing that's happened to you.

He felt frustrated, helpless and vulnerable, his emotions raw and exposed before the critical eye of his conscience. He shouldn't have said those things to her, but he had been so angry at Carole that he had taken his frustrations out on Rae.

Go after her.

No! Dammit, it's a matter of pride. I've had my fill of women lately. They only complicate my life.

Jonathan glanced through the open study door at the staircase. He had to see his mother and that was a conversation he dreaded more than anything. Maybe if he talked with Carole one more time. No, he wasn't a fool. He knew when he was beat.

But aren't you a fool, King?

Even though the sun was setting, the dark blue sky streaked red-orange, the air was oppressive, the heat of the July day stifling. Rae sought shelter under a towering oak that afforded a visitor to Woodward Park some comfort.

Sitting down on the grass near the wall that separated the park from the Rose Garden, Rae breathed in the smells of the intoxicating varieties of roses. A sea of color stretched out before her with rows of red, yellow, white and pink flowers.

This was such a beautiful, peaceful place in the middle of a large, growing city. Whenever Rae faced a big decision she always found herself sitting cross-legged on this bed of grass, staring at her favorite flower as though the roses had the answer.

Vivid memories leaped into her mind of white rosebuds on her desk, then later full-blossomed, blood-red roses. Jonathan had been right. Until he had entered her world, she had only been living half a life.

These last few weeks she had been fighting her feelings for Jonathan harder than she had fought him over Hamilton Oil. Last night she had given up the battle. She loved him deeply, wholly.

Well, now that you have admitted that to yourself what are you going to do about it?

Instantly Rae knew the answer to that question. *Fight!* She had never given up before. No one could ever call her a quitter and she had no intention of doing it now.

If she got hurt in the process, at least it was better than the cold, empty life she had been leading before Jonathan had barged his way into her world. She had never felt so exhilarated as when she fought with him, made love with him, or simply enjoyed his sharp wit and stimulating conversation. Life with him would be exciting and challenging, never dull.

First she would go back to her apartment and change into something feminine—not the jeans she wore now. Then she would go back to his home and make him see reason. She would tell him that she loved him. The hell with her pride!

With a plan of action mapped out in her mind, Rae closed her eyes for a few minutes to absorb the tranquility of her surroundings. The sounds of a child's laughter, a bird singing, a couple's murmured voices drifted to her ears, and all of her earlier anxiety ebbed.

Finally at peace with herself, Rae stood and made her way to her car. Directing her sedan toward her apartment she remembered the couple in the park sitting on a bench, holding hands, eyes only for each other. That vision gave her the needed courage to carry out her campaign. It wouldn't be long before she faced Jonathan with the truth.

Outside Rae's apartment Carole leaned against her front door holding a bouquet of two dozen white roses. Puzzlement puckered Rae's brown.

Carole quickly explained, "I haven't resorted to sending you flowers. A delivery boy was here about ten minutes ago and I told him I would see that you got them. From Jonathan?" Curiosity bathed Carole's expression. "What happened after I left?"

"That's not important. What's important is you."

Rae opened the door to her apartment, taking the crystal vase from Carole as she moved inside. Instinctively Rae knew who had sent them and why. Her spirits soared.

"Well, aren't you going to look at the card? The suspense is killing me."

"I can see you won't tell me why you've come until I do."

Rae slid the white card from its envelope, her hands trembling slightly as she read.

I'm sorry, babe.

My love always,

Jonathan

Those simple words seared into her mind and would stay with her forever. Tears filled her eyes and Rae blinked them away. There was still a lot to be settled, but the future suddenly looked bright.

"I gather brother dear finally got smart."

"Cut the wisecracks, Carole. Right now I would say you should concentrate fully on your own problem. Why did you come here?" Rae's voice was firm as she motioned for Carole to have a seat, but her expression was gentle, understanding.

Carole hesitated for a few seconds, then sat on the couch, her hands twisted together in her lap. "I needed someone to talk to and not many of my friends are very sensible and levelheaded like you. I'm so confused. I don't know what to do. I've never had to make any difficult decisions before and this one is a lulu."

"What do *you* really want to do?"

"That's the problem. I'm not sure. I've never had much practice in weighing the pros and cons like Jonathan. If you were I, what would you do?"

"Oh, no, you don't. I'm not you, Carole. What I would do wouldn't necessarily be best for you. Do you love Bradley?"

Carole's tensed body sagged back against the cushions, a frown on her face. "I don't want anyone to run my life anymore. I don't want to move from Jonathan's control to Bradley's. I'm scared, Rae. I want my freedom, but I'm not handling it very well."

"Do you love Bradley?"

"Yes. Yes!"

"Does he know you're pregnant with his child?"

Carole's cynicism showed on her face. "I'm sure Jonathan has told him by now."

"Don't paint your brother all black. I grant you he has made some mistakes with you, but you've given him your permission by always running home to him to solve anything that was the least bit hard for you to deal with."

"I did try to tell Jonathan I was pregnant on Friday, but he wouldn't listen. He told me to take care of my own problems for once. I got angry at him and went to Mother." Carole smoothed her hair away from her face with jerky movements. "I'm not proud of that."

"Don't you think you should be discussing this with Bradley? Today a pregnancy can usually be prevented. Maybe you wanted to become pregnant subconsciously so the decision of marrying Bradley would be made for you. Think that over and talk with Bradley.

He deserves to at least know you're carrying his child."

For a long moment Carole was lost in deep thought before she rose, a smile clearing the confusion from her face. "Thank you, Rae. I hope you'll become my sister-in-law. I haven't been very independent or strong, but maybe with you as an example I can learn. I'll have that talk with Bradley. Jonathan and Bradley are different. Bradley never thought for one minute of me as a younger sister," Carole said with a laugh, walking toward the front door.

The minute the door closed behind Carole, Rae whirled around and headed for her bedroom. She tore off her tank top and jeans, then began sifting through her wardrobe for the right dress.

Finally she settled on a burnt-orange sundress with thin spaghetti straps, a soft-looking full skirt that came to the middle of her knees and a scooped neckline that offered a glimpse of her breasts.

A current of excited tension traveled through her with the speed of electricity through wires. Samuel, the butler, admitted her into the house, telling her Mrs. King was asleep and that Mr. King was in his study.

Rae rapped softly at the study door, her courage starting to waver when she heard nothing from within. Hesitantly she opened the door, the room in total darkness.

"Come in," spoke a gruff voice from the dark shadows.

"Jonathan?"

A lamp clicked on, illuminating the room in a soft golden glow.

"Rae! I wasn't sure you would come." Jonathan sat in an overstuffed chair, an unfinished drink in his hand. He held the glass up and continued, "I had every intention of getting roaring drunk, but I've decided that that wouldn't be an answer to my problem or my needs."

"What problem?" Rae asked, shutting the door behind her, her pulse accelerating at the pure sensual look in Jonathan's eyes.

"You!"

"What needs?"

"You!"

Rae walked to where Jonathan was sitting and knelt in front of him. A radiant smile declared to him her love, all her feelings clearly visible in her expression as she grasped his hand and held it to her cheek.

"I love you, Jonathan King."

Turning his hand, Rae kissed the palm, then each fingertip.

"And I love you, Rae Hamilton. Do you think it's possible for two very stubborn, proud people to marry and make the marriage work?"

"If that's a back-door proposal, I accept, Jonathan King. Haven't you figured out by now I don't give up? That very stubbornness and pride we both have will be what makes our marriage last. Neither one of us will ever want to admit we've failed."

"I suppose you're right. Apologies don't

come easily to us. But when I apologize I mean it."

Jonathan drew Rae up onto his lap and nuzzled her neck. She moved slightly away to look into the smoldering fires of his eyes, then lower, her gaze resting upon his finely chiseled lips, so close to her mouth that his breath tingled her cheek.

"A bouquet of white roses will do nicely as a starter," she said breathlessly right before he took her mouth with a passionate need only she could satisfy.

From that moment on Rae was lost to the world of reality. Their eyes, mouth and hands couldn't seem to get enough of each other as they pledged their love with their actions. Even if he hadn't said he loved her earlier, Rae would have known. His body spoke the silent message over and over as they came together, meeting as a man and woman equally sharing in a blissful ecstasy only possible because of the other.

Later, as Rae lay within Jonathan's embrace on the couch, she toyed with the fine hairs on his chest. "Jonathan, what are you going to do about *Hamilton* Oil?" She hadn't meant to put the emphasis on Hamilton, but she had.

"What do you want me to do, Rae?"

His tone told her nothing, his expression neutral. What did *she* want? She had fought him so long on this that she had asked the question without really thinking through her revised feelings.

"I want to manage Hamilton Oil, Jonathan, *but* I know now I still have a few things to learn from you."

"Not many, baby. During the next few months I'm going to be busy moving some of my operation back to Tulsa. You're going to have to manage without me. I'll always be here to give you advice, but you're a quick learner, Rae."

A rush of trust and a sense of belonging to someone totally warmed her. "You're willing to let me buy your controlling interest?" Rae sat up, her eyes wide with mock disbelief.

"You heard me. Besides, it will all be in the family."

15-Day Free Trial Offer
6 Silhouette Romances

6 Silhouette Romances, free for 15 days! We'll send you 6 new Silhouette Romances to keep for 15 days, absolutely free! If you decide not to keep them, send them back to us. You pay nothing.

Free Home Delivery. But if you enjoy them as much as we think you will, keep them by paying the invoice enclosed with your free trial shipment. We'll pay all shipping and handling charges. You get the convenience of Home Delivery and we pay the postage and handling charge each month.

Don't miss a copy. The Silhouette Book Club is the way to make sure you'll be able to receive every new romance we publish before they're sold out. There is no minimum number of books to buy and you can cancel at any time.

This offer expires July 31, 1984

Silhouette Book Club, Dept. SRSE 7L
120 Brighton Road, Clifton, NJ 07012

Please send me 6 Silhouette Romances to keep for 15 days, absolutely free. I understand I am not obligated to join the Silhouette Book Club unless I decide to keep them.

NAME _____

ADDRESS _____

CITY _____ STATE _____ ZIP _____

MORE ROMANCE FOR
A SPECIAL WAY TO RELAX

$1.95 each

2 ☐ Hastings	23 ☐ Charles	45 ☐ Charles	66 ☐ Mikels
3 ☐ Dixon	24 ☐ Dixon	46 ☐ Howard	67 ☐ Shaw
4 ☐ Vitek	25 ☐ Hardy	47 ☐ Stephens	68 ☐ Sinclair
5 ☐ Converse	26 ☐ Scott	48 ☐ Ferrell	69 ☐ Dalton
6 ☐ Douglass	27 ☐ Wisdom	49 ☐ Hastings	70 ☐ Clare
7 ☐ Stanford	28 ☐ Ripy	50 ☐ Browning	71 ☐ Skillern
8 ☐ Halston	29 ☐ Bergen	51 ☐ Trent	72 ☐ Belmont
9 ☐ Baxter	30 ☐ Stephens	52 ☐ Sinclair	73 ☐ Taylor
10 ☐ Thiels	31 ☐ Baxter	53 ☐ Thomas	74 ☐ Wisdom
11 ☐ Thornton	32 ☐ Douglass	54 ☐ Hohl	75 ☐ John
12 ☐ Sinclair	33 ☐ Palmer	55 ☐ Stanford	76 ☐ Ripy
13 ☐ Beckman	35 ☐ James	56 ☐ Wallace	77 ☐ Bergen
14 ☐ Keene	36 ☐ Dailey	57 ☐ Thornton	78 ☐ Gladstone
15 ☐ James	37 ☐ Stanford	58 ☐ Douglass	79 ☐ Hastings
16 ☐ Carr	38 ☐ John	59 ☐ Roberts	80 ☐ Douglass
17 ☐ John	39 ☐ Milan	60 ☐ Thorne	81 ☐ Thornton
18 ☐ Hamilton	40 ☐ Converse	61 ☐ Beckman	82 ☐ McKenna
19 ☐ Shaw	41 ☐ Halston	62 ☐ Bright	83 ☐ Major
20 ☐ Musgrave	42 ☐ Drummond	63 ☐ Wallace	84 ☐ Stephens
21 ☐ Hastings	43 ☐ Shaw	64 ☐ Converse	85 ☐ Beckman
22 ☐ Howard	44 ☐ Eden	65 ☐ Cates	86 ☐ Halston

Silhouette Special Edition

87 ☐ Dixon	101 ☐ Bergen	115 ☐ Halston	129 ☐ Rowe
88 ☐ Saxon	102 ☐ Wallace	116 ☐ Roberts	130 ☐ Carr
89 ☐ Meriwether	103 ☐ Taylor	117 ☐ Converse	131 ☐ Lee
90 ☐ Justin	104 ☐ Wallace	118 ☐ Jackson	132 ☐ Dailey
91 ☐ Stanford	105 ☐ Sinclair	119 ☐ Langan	133 ☐ Douglass
92 ☐ Hamilton	106 ☐ John	120 ☐ Dixon	134 ☐ Ripy
93 ☐ Lacey	107 ☐ Ross	121 ☐ Shaw	135 ☐ Seger
94 ☐ Barrie	108 ☐ Stephens	122 ☐ Walker	136 ☐ Scott
95 ☐ Doyle	109 ☐ Beckman	123 ☐ Douglass	137 ☐ Parker
96 ☐ Baxter	110 ☐ Browning	124 ☐ Mikels	138 ☐ Thornton
97 ☐ Shaw	111 ☐ Thorne	125 ☐ Cates	
98 ☐ Hurley	112 ☐ Belmont	126 ☐ Wildman	
99 ☐ Dixon	113 ☐ Camp	127 ☐ Taylor	
100 ☐ Roberts	114 ☐ Ripy	128 ☐ Macomber	

LOOK FOR *SHINING HOUR* BY PAT WALLACE
AVAILABLE IN FEBRUARY AND
A LOVESONG AND YOU BY LINDA SHAW
IN MARCH.

SILHOUETTE SPECIAL EDITION, Department SE/2
1230 Avenue of the Americas
New York, NY 10020

Please send me the books I have checked above. I am enclosing $_____
(please add 75¢ to cover postage and handling. NYS and NYC residents please
add appropriate sales tax). Send check or money order—no cash or C.O.D.'s
please. Allow six weeks for delivery.

NAME _____

ADDRESS _____

CITY _____ STATE/ZIP _____